DEMOLISHED

CATHRYN FOX

COPYRIGHT

Demolished
Copyright 2020 by Cathryn Fox
Published by Cathryn Fox

ISBN Ebook: 978-1-989374-15-3
ISBN Print: 978-1-989374-16-0

SUMMER

Cheeseburger halfway to my mouth, I sink farther into the crispy vinyl booth and glance at the diner door for the hundredth time. *Relax. He doesn't know where you are.* I suck in a quick breath and exhale slowly to calm myself, then tear into my meal like it is the first of the day, which, of course, it is. No time to eat when you're on the run from Southern California to Blue Bay, Connecticut.

I dip my greasy fry into the ketchup and toss it into my mouth, my stomach rebelling after being hollow for so long. As I chew, I do another slow sweep of the near-empty establishment, avoiding eye contact with the sleazy guy in the corner who keeps staring at me over the rim of his tumbler. I can't help but wonder if he's the Dick in "Dick's Driving Inn and Diner" on Route 5. Talk about the perfect name for a seedy, out-of-the-way hotel.

The sound of rusty hinges groaning in protest draws my focus and my gaze flies back to the heavy wooden door in time to see it swing open. It hits the wall with a thud and my heart jumps into my throat when I glimpse the tower of solid muscle walking into the place like he owns it. *No way.* I blink, sure I'm hallucinating. But when I open my eyes again, there is no mistaking the man darkening the doorway. *Sean Owens.* Blue Bay's poster boy for authority issues, and the man who put the "O" in Owens. Not that I know that firsthand. I don't. But what I do know is he's the toughest, roughest guy from my childhood, and lethal to me in entirely different ways.

I swallow my fry, and drop the grease-soaked bun onto the plate, my attention now on the beautifully sculpted face that I'd recognize even if I hadn't been watching him on the motocross circuit for years with my dad—before his death six months ago. Would Sean recognize me, too? I sure as hell hope not. After overhearing my ex-boyfriend on the phone, and discovering my life is in danger, I have no idea who I can trust. My father's warning words ring in my ears—*Trust no one.*

But this is Sean Owens. Blue Bay's hottest, sexiest motocross racer who always circled me in a bubble of safety when I was a kid.

Dressed in a leather jacket that had to be custom made to fit those broad shoulders and hewn muscles, he rakes thick dark hair from his face, those big strong arms of his gaining my attention. I remember those arms, the way they'd pulled me from the water when I'd nearly drowned.

My focus moves to his mouth, to lips that quirk at the waitress as he walks up to the bar and throws one solid, jean-clad thigh over the stool. He moves with a grace a man his size shouldn't possess. Unable to tear my gaze away, I look him over. His hair is too long. Unruly. Like him. And those lips. God, those lips. I once felt them moving over mine, but at fourteen years old, when he was giving me mouth-to-mouth, I was far too young to appreciate them fully. After that near-drowning incident I followed him around like a lovesick puppy. But being two years my senior—a hot, legendary troublemaker who tore up the side streets on his motorbike—I could never catch him.

He drops down onto the stool, a tense, restless energy about him, as he orders a beer. It arrives, and he takes a long pull from the bottle, gulping it back like he's had a hell of a day. I can relate. The bottle hits the bar with a thud. He twirls it, then slowly raises his head like he senses me staring. Heavy, pensive eyes turn on me, and a bolt of heat rushes through my body, lighting up every erogenous zone along the way.

What the hell? How can I be aroused at a time like this?

I look away and bite into my soggy hamburger, even though my appetite has long ago raced out of the diner. As my throat tightens, I swallow and reach for my soda to wash down the lump.

"Can I buy you a drink?"

A body shadows my table. I glance up to see the creepy guy from the corner standing over me. He takes a swig from his tumbler, and moves closer. His stale breath falls over me, and my gag reflex kicks in.

"No, I'm good," I say, swallowing again in an effort to keep my dinner from making a second appearance.

He sways, the amber liquid in his glass spilling over the sides. "Come on," he insists, his voice slurring. "Let me buy you a drink."

I gesture toward my soda. "I already have a drink." I let my hair fall forward to avoid eye contact, and silently will him to leave. It doesn't work. The shadow over my table grows, thickens, claws at me as he rocks against the brass ledge. Metal table legs shift on the grimy floor and I cringe as the sound goes right through me. I continue to ignore him but he still doesn't get the hint.

"Yeah, but a pretty little thing like you should never drink alone."

A stool squeaks, followed by heavy motorcycle boots thudding on the cracked and pitted floor. The sound of each stomp roars like a souped-up two stroke in my ears as Mr. Sex in a Leather Jacket winds his way around a few tables. An intoxicating scent of the open road and something uniquely Sean permeates the air with each determined slide, chasing away the foul scent of whiskey and sadness.

Sean stops behind the man, towers over him. "Take off."

"Wha—" The guy turns, stumbles a bit, and squares off against Sean. Clearly alcohol has impaired his judgment. Either that or he has a death wish. Not that I think Sean will deck the guy. The fight wouldn't be fair, and while Blue Bay's toughest bad boy has trouble written all over him, I don't take him for the kind of guy who likes to play dirty. At least not outside the bedroom.

Stop thinking about Sean and sex.

A muscle in Sean's jaw ticks, so tense I fear it could snap out of place. "I said take off."

Stale breath grumbles, "I just got here, man."

Even in the dimly lit bar, I can see Sean's green eyes darken.

"And now you're leaving."

The creep's gaze bounces back and forth between Sean and me like he's some kind of bobblehead. "What, is she with you?"

Sean's gaze slides to mine and holds. Dark. Dangerous. Sensual. "Yeah, she's with me."

The guy shifts from one foot to the other and glares at Sean. Sean stands deathly still. His big hands, one still holding a beer bottle, sit idle at his sides—a contradiction to his predatory stance, the tightness in his jaw. A wild wolf poised to pounce.

Damn . . .

The creep must realize the danger before him. He turns, grunts something unintelligible and slinks back to his stool.

"Thank you," I murmur and lower my head, hoping Sean will take the hint and walk back to the bar. He stands there, silent for a long agonizing minute, towering over me like six feet of pure testosterone. My stomach flutters at the weight of his gaze.

Double damn.

"You lost?"

Lost? No, but I can get why he's asking me that. I'm dressed in my usual work clothes—all I could grab at a moment's notice—and this establishment is one up from a dive, a place I wouldn't normally frequent. All the more reason for me to stay here. Never in a million would my ex think to look for me at Dick's Driving Inn on Route 5. Yet here is Sean—his body broken and scarred from years on the circuit—hovering close and making me feel safe, yet vulnerable, a mixed bag of emotions that is confusing my thoughts. As a frisson of nervousness prowls through my blood, I lift my head, meeting his crotch face on.

"Ah . . . no. Not lost," I manage to get out. Damn, way to sound convincing. But how the hell am I supposed to pull off composed when I'm staring at his package, which just happens to be bundled tightly in worn jeans that hug him in all the right ways. A garbled noise sounds in my throat and I disguise it with a cough and lift my head, forcing my eyes to his.

Pull yourself together, girl.

He scrubs his chin, and I like the sound it makes. In fact, I like everything about this guy. Always have. He stares at me for a moment, his gaze dark, scrutinizing. Something flashes in his eyes. Is it recognition? As a sliver of dread takes hold, I shift in my seat, the vinyl crackling beneath my backside. I glance heavenward and give a silent prayer. Please don't let him remember me. Not that I think he, or anyone in Blue Bay will recognize me now, which is one of the reasons I chose the seaside location as a hideout—that, and of course, the key to the cottage was in a lockbox Dad had given me months ago. Heck, it's been thirteen long years since my family and I summered in the once sleepy town, and I'm no longer the gangly little pigtailed blonde with sun-kissed freckles. Well, that's not entirely true. I still have the freckles. But my hair has darkened over time and my once lanky, boylike body has grown curves. Today I'm the antithesis of that young girl, completely unrecognizable to the townsfolk—to Sean.

After Mom's death, the winter just before I turned fifteen, Dad and I boarded the place up, locking years of fond memories behind lumber and nails. We never talked about the place, yet Dad couldn't bring himself to sell it. Now, with limited funds and resources for survival, I'm glad that he kept it in the family.

Sean shifts his stance to catalog the room. I almost breathe a sigh of relief when my face is no longer inches from his crotch. Almost. Because now I'm one-on-one with his ass, and oh what a perfect ass it is.

"You don't sound too sure about that," he says, his voice deeper, more grown up, despite his strikingly boyish good looks.

"Positive," I counter, injecting more assurance into my voice as I drag my focus from his perfect backside. "I'm just passing through on my way to catch up with an old girlfriend."

"Girlfriend?"

"She's a girl and a friend, I'm not . . ."

He grins and takes another long pull from his bottle. A drop of beer forms on his mouth, and he swipes his tongue over his bottom lip. My thighs quiver, and it's all I can do not to spread them and tell him to take me already.

"Yeah, I'm just passing through, too," he says.

Chances are he's on his way to another motocross event. Good. Right now I don't need the distraction of Sean. Not when my life is in danger. No, right now I need to hide out, and figure out where my father hid a ledger that my ex Jack wants so badly he's willing to hurt me for it? Jack is a United States naval officer and served under my father for years, and he has way more resources and connections than I do so I really shouldn't be talking to anyone, or drawing any kind of attention to myself. By rights, I should end this conversation with Sean right now, get in my truck and drive straight through the night until I reach the boarded-up cottage.

Sean leans closer, crowding me. "Is that your truck out there?"

"Ah, why?" Does he need a lift or something?

"Just asking." He shrugs, his gaze dropping to my mouth. He fixates on it as his voice slides across the shell of my ear, the heat behind it speaking volumes. O-kay . . .

Obviously I should have gone with the *something*, because clearly it's not a lift he's after. No, what he wants from me is far more intimate, and teases parts of my body that have been dormant for too long. Yeah, that's right, dormant. Closed off. Inactive. Total hibernation.

The truth is, I've dated Jack for six months—he practically lived at my condo toward the end of it—but we hadn't been intimate in a long time. I'd wanted to break it off. Tried to break it off, actually. But he clung, refusing to let me go. He must have sensed my restlessness and impatience with the relationship; otherwise he wouldn't be ready to "apply pressure to get the ledger once and for all." His words, not mine—ones I overheard during a private phone conversation he was having with God knows who. I have no idea where that ledger is, or what information it contains. All I know is I need to keep a low profile and find it before he does. Even though my dad's death was ruled an accident, my gut tells me otherwise. If Jack is willing to hurt me to get answers, what the hell did he do to my father?

At first it stung to learn that Jack had been using me all this time. But as soon as I clued in to what "apply pressure" meant, fear quickly overrode pride. Perhaps the hurt, the betrayal, and fear are the reasons I'm so affected by Sean. Or perhaps it's simply because this is Sean.

Images of me between the sheets with the stack of muscle towering close, his protective hands shaping my body as he reacquaints those sensuous lips with mine rush through me. I tremble. Why shouldn't I go for it? Why shouldn't I forget about the real world and lose myself in him for a few short hours. I ignore the million reasons clanging around inside my head, and stare at his big hands as they push his hair from his forehead, a familiar habit.

"Yeah, it's my truck," I finally say.

"You're a long way from home."

I freeze for a second, then relax. My license plate says California. It doesn't mean he knows me. "Like I said, I'm on my way to visit an old friend."

"Kind of a big truck for a small girl to drive halfway around the country, don't you think?"

Yeah, I do. Too big and too noticeable. But I had no choice. My car was in the shop and my father's truck was the only thing available when I needed to flee.

"I like things big," I shoot back, not really sure why I'm going on the defense, but as soon as the words leave my mouth, I scramble to get them back. Good God, why don't I just come out and tell him that I want to have sex with him, I silently scoff. Like he doesn't already know. I've been eye fucking him since he walked into the place.

The corner of his mouth quirks and a dimple forms. Oh, that dimple. So ridiculously sexy I can barely stand it. "Oh, yeah?" He leans down and whispers against my temple, bathing my skin in warmth and sensual awareness: "Want to get out of here? Go someplace and get something decent to eat?"

His soft words melt my body and brain, not great at a time when I need to think with clarity. My survival depends on it and I have no idea who I can trust.

This is Sean.

I'm not naïve enough to believe it's a decent meal he's after, and as fight-or-flight instincts kick in I take in his raw strength, revel in the energy arcing between us. Heat floods my core, but my brain yells at me to say no.

"Yeah, okay," I murmur, shocking myself. A one-night stand is so uncharacteristic of me. Then again, I've been doing a lot of things I've never done before.

I make a move to get up, but he cups my elbow and pulls me from my seat. My body molds against his, and his warmth envelopes me. I sag into him, a false sense of comfort overcoming me, something I haven't felt in the last six months, ever since my late father handed me a metal lockbox containing a huge amount of cash, the key to the Blue Bay cottage, and fake identification . . . just in case.

Just in case *what?*

I didn't ask. Didn't think to. Danger isn't a part of my world. I'm a chiropractor, for God's sake. The only threat I face comes in the form of a malpractice suit, and that hasn't happened yet. How could my father possibly think I'd know what to do when faced with danger? I've never walked in his shoes, don't even know the rules.

That's why my first instinct was to run after hearing my life was in danger. I didn't know who to trust or even if I'd be safe going to the police. My ex has a lot of connections, so I just bolted and headed for Blue Bay. Is it possible my father hid the ledger somewhere in the small town? I'm not convinced, since we never talked about the cottage after boarding it up, and it was far too painful to return. But for now, until I can figure out my next move, it's the safest place I know.

"You okay?" he asks, his breath hot, distracting against my neck.

I study him. God, he is so beautiful. Dark eyes framed by thick lashes, a square jaw dusted with a day's worth of stubble. A hint of a tattoo flirts with the base of his collar, and I feel a tug low in my pelvis. Tough. Rough. The epitome of maleness. Pleasure unfurls inside me.

"Yeah, sure." I try for casual and extricate myself from his arms, but instantly miss his warmth, his big arms around me.

He pulls me back, and his erection presses against my stomach. My sex clenches so hard I'm sure if I squeeze my legs together I'll orgasm. I muffle a cry of pleasure, aching for him to touch me, to slide his hands into my panties and make me forget the real world for a few hours. I suck in a breath, shocked at the intensity of my responses.

His eyes never leave mine. "Then let's get out of here."

My pulse pounds at the base of my throat. Leaving with him is stupid. Reckless. But after running for days, who could blame me for wanting to feel comfort in his arms, to feel safe for just one night. It isn't rational, or smart, but fear is causing me to do unwise things, like fall into bed with a boy from my past when I'm on the way to a town where no one knows my name.

2

SEAN

Summer Wheeler.

All grown up.

I can hardly believe I'm walking out of a Dick's Inn and Diner—and hopefully into one of its rooms—with sweet Summer Wheeler, the girl I've always crushed on but couldn't do anything about. Christ, back in the day two years might as well have been a chasm, but today, not so much.

Jesus, she's gorgeous. Has lush curves that every guy's dreams are made of. Her once blond hair is now as dark as the night sky, rich, luxurious, citrus scented, and damned if I can't wait to see those curls spill across my pillow. She still has that sprinkling of freckles on her nose that make her look young and adorable, and those lips . . . Goddammit, never have I seen lips that were so plush, so damn kissable. A bolt of lust hits like a sucker punch, and my body trembles, anxious to taste her heat, to discover what she's wearing under her professional clothes. Fuck, it's all I can do not to back her up against that big truck of hers and take her right outside in the parking lot.

Yeah, sure, I'm supposed to be getting my shit together,

turning over a new leaf, becoming a productive, upstanding citizen of Blue Bay and every other stupid fucking idiomatic expression that meant I needed to do better for my family. But I'm not in Blue Bay yet, headed back to a place where everyone knows my name—and the cops don't like me—to take over my dad's construction business. Yup, I get it, it's time to step into the role I'd been groomed for since I could hold a hammer, and spend less time on the road satisfying my own selfish urges. When I get home I'll be on the straight and narrow: no women, no distractions, and no trouble with the law.

Until then, however . . .

I put my hand on the small of her back and the heat that fires between us is almost catastrophic. Jesus. Who'd have thought that after all these years there'd still be such a powerful pull? I shake my head. Chemistry like this doesn't come along every day.

The warm night air falls over us as I push the lounge door open and guide her into the night. I pause and glance up and down the long strip of black street. I'd been in this Podunk town in the past, circling through as I went from one sponsored motocross event to the next. Hell, all I need is a place to lay my head, but seriously what is Summer really doing in a shit place like this? Designer clothes. Expensive truck. She is so out of her element. Where exactly is she headed, and who is this friend she's visiting? More importantly, why is she pretending she doesn't know me?

I'm pretty good at reading people and I spotted the recognition flashing in her whiskey-colored eyes the second I met them. Then again, maybe she doesn't want to acknowledge me because . . . well . . . because for her, this is just a quick hot affair as she passes through town. Fine, if she wants to play it that way, I can, too. No names. Anonymous sex.

This isn't my first rodeo and all cards on the table, it's for the best. I don't have time for more.

"This town doesn't have much, but there's a pizza joint two blocks down. It's decent." Her dark lashes flash over darker eyes, meeting my gaze straight on. She doesn't even look like she's breathing, which gives me the distinct impression that this isn't something she does on a regular basis. I brush my knuckles along her arm, and she shivers. "Unless you'd prefer to just—"

"I'd prefer," she whispers.

My cock throbs. Apparently little Sean prefers that, too. I pull a key card from my back pocket, and the letter stuffed inside nearly falls out. I shove it back, not wanting to think about the stabbing pain behind each written—and unwritten —word. Later I'll wallow in my own misery, kick my stupid fucked-up ass, and condemn myself for my selfish ways. Christ knows there'll be plenty of time for that in the coming months.

"My room or yours?" I ask.

She grins at the cheesy comment, the tension easing a bit from her body. "Yours."

Interesting. Here I thought she'd pick hers, the familiarity of the personal belongings she'd brought with her giving her a level of comfort. Then again maybe she chose mine so she could slip out under the cover of darkness. No awkward goodbyes. No stilted morning conversation.

My hand brushes hers as I lean in to give her a nudge in the right direction. Her steps are slow, cautious. Is she having second thoughts? Her nervousness gives me pause. For fuck's sake, this is Summer Wheeler. Not some groupie on the circuit eager to sleep with every winning rider. I probably shouldn't have come on so strong. But the fact is I've thought about her so much over the years, knew she'd grow into a beautiful woman. The second I saw her sitting all alone at the table, I wanted her in the worst fucking way. I stop, turn to her and note the way her lashes are fluttering rapidly, a guardedness about her as apprehension flashes over her face. My stomach plummets.

"If you don't—"

"I . . ." Her hand goes to my chest, the warmth of her fingers seeping under my T-shirt. I move closer, joining our bodies, and press a leg between hers. Her heat is like an electrical jolt to my cock. Fuck, if she says no, it just might kill me. "I do," she whispers on a rushed breath. An undeniable sense of relief that I don't want to think too much about moves through me and I put my hand on her face. My thumb brushes her bottom lip. Her skin is so fucking soft, her mouth so damn tempting, I can't wait another second.

Giving in to impulse I dip my head, and my lips go to hers. She parts for me, welcoming me inside. I taste her. Savor her sweetness. Sweet fuck. I knew she'd taste good, but not this good. I breathe in the scent of her skin, pull it deep into my lungs. The air grows thick, gets hot, and vibrates with volatile sexual awareness

I drag her closer, and the feel of her breasts, her hard nipples against my chest, short-circuits my brain, and makes me forget we're still outside. I push my knee deeper between her legs, and pull her down to rub my thigh against her pussy. Her legs squeeze mine, the friction torturing my throbbing cock.

"Fuck," I murmur into her mouth as a strange possessiveness rages inside me. Maybe it's because I've wanted to kiss her like this for so goddamn long. "I need you naked."

She moans. "Yes, please."

A car door slams and I shift gears, needing to get her inside so I can have her all to myself and do wicked things to her body. I wrap my hand around her waist, and usher her to my door. Her breath is coming quicker now, matching mine, and the second I get her into my room, I slam the door shut, lock it behind us, and position her against it.

I taste her again, fuck her mouth with my tongue, and the moan that sounds in the depths of her throat does something strange to me. I push her hair back and thrust my tongue deeper inside her mouth, wanting to taste every bit of her. Sweat breaks out on my forehead, my body so tight with restraint, my muscles rebel. She writhes, and I grab her hands, forcing them over her head, needing her at my mercy.

She gasps, as I hold both of her small hands in one of mine, the other going to her curves. I trail my hand down her sides, outlining the swell of one breast and she pushes against me. She's so damn responsive it's enough to make me go insane. Her breath comes out in a labored burst, as she arches in to me.

"You want me?" I ask.

"Yes." Her hot breath falls over my neck.

"Tell me."

She gasps like she's struggling for air and my veins surge with desire. "I want you."

"Bad enough to let me take you rough and hard, the way I need to take you?"

"Oh, God."

"Yeah, you can pray, baby. But I plan to make you shatter all around me."

"I . . . ," she murmurs, her words falling off, like she could no longer form a sentence.

"You'll break so hard, baby, you'll think you're in a downpour, naked and quivering as I have my way with you." I run my tongue over her bottom lip and inch back. "Tell me you want that."

Her throat ripples as she swallowed. "I want that," she rushes out on a breathless whisper.

I slip my hands into her pants, shoving my way into her

panties. *Fuck me.* I feel like someone just set dynamite off in my head when I find her so hot and wet for me. I part her folds, and slowly circle her clit. She cries out in ecstasy, and jerks her hips forward.

"Please . . . ," she begs, so hot for it. Her lashes flutter, color spreads across her cheeks. "I need . . . I haven't . . ." I don't miss the desperate edge to her voice before it falls off. Christ, when was the last fucking time someone touched her?

"Easy, baby," I say, more determined than ever to make this good for her. "I'm going to give you what you want."

Fire blazes through me and I breathe slow and deep to keep a measure control, even though I can feel it slipping away. I stroke her swollen clit, slowly drag my finger over it, and her heat burns through me. Her mouth opens but no words form, turning me on even more. Watching her come undone is so fucking sexy.

She leans forward, runs her tongue over the scars on my throat and I nearly break. Fuck. I push a finger insider her and she whimpers. Want ripples through me with such force I can barely think straight. I push a second finger in and my cock jumps, aching to switch places with my hand.

I still my hand inside her and her eyes flash open. "Don't stop."

"Ride my fingers. Show me how much you want my cock."

Her hips move shamelessly, a girl taking what she needs. Fucking sexy. She gyrates, grinding with an urgency that sends electrical charges through me. She grows wetter, slicker with each pump, and my mouth waters, wanting a taste. Her pulse throbs wildly at the base of her neck and with my fingers still inside her, I press my lips to her throat. Her entire body quakes.

I let her hands go and they fall to my shoulders, her touch like fire on my skin. Her fingernails drag skin as she rocks into me, her pussy tightening around my fingers as her climax mounts.

"I'm . . . Oh, yes . . ."

I drop to my knees, none too gently drag her pants down, and bury my face between her legs. I lick, nibble, and bite at her like a starved predator who's just taken down his prey. Ravenous, greedy, I take her clit into my mouth and suck so hard, she grabs the back of my head and bucks against me. Her body trembles, and her pussy swells. My throat dries and I moan my approval, desperate to hydrate myself with her juices. Thirsty for a taste, I brush my fingers over the hot bundles of nerves inside her, and press hot openmouthed kisses to her pussy.

A cry rips from her, and she clenches hard around my finger. I thrust into her again, and try to drag air into my lungs as her hot juices drip down my hand.

"Yes," she whimpers, moving against my fingers and riding out the sweet sensations. I slide up her body, and when her pussy stops trembling, she crumbles against me. I scoop her up, carry her to the bed and set her on the edge. Dim eyes full of want stare up at me as I shrug out of my jacket and tug my T-shirt over my shoulders. Dark eyes widen as she takes in my scars. I'm used to it. In fact most women are turned on by it, but not Summer. No, her eyes are filled with concern. Fucking worry.

Time slows for a minute, the seconds between heartbeats lengthening, stretching, a slow drag, a hard thump. I suck in a sharp breath to kick-start it, then clench down on my back teeth hard enough to crack them.

"I'm fine," I say, my voice coming out harder than I intended.

She reaches for me, and I touch her shoulders and force her down on her knees. "I'm going to fuck your mouth." I rip open my pants and free my cock. Yeah, I'm big, and my size shocks most women. But not Summer. She licks her lips like she's eager to take every inch of me. *Jesus.*

I step into her, take my cock into my hand and stroke it. Not to get it ready. I've been ready since we were teens. Summer wets her lush mouth. Hot and possessive, she leans forward and draws me in as deeply as possible. Her other hand goes to my balls, and they draw up as she massages. I pull her hair back, and nearly shoot down her throat when I find her glancing up at me, her eyes dark, sexy, enjoying every second of this as much as I am.

She twirls her tongue around my crown, and dips into the precum. My veins fill with heated blood, and she presses her tongue to them. The soft, sexy moan of pleasure is pretty much more than I can take. I grip her shoulders, draw her up and nudge her until she's sitting on the bed.

"Naked. Now."

I stand perfectly still, watching, waiting as her fingers work her blouse. Impatience runs through me and I'm seconds from tearing her shirt wide open when she eases it from her shoulders. My gaze drops to her black lace bra. *Black lace bra.* Kill me fucking now.

She reaches behind her back, unhooks it and lets it fall to the floor. My gaze zeroes in on the most perfect breasts I've ever set eyes on. Pale nipples, hard, sweet, beckoning my mouth. Who am I to disappoint?

I kick my pants and shorts off and drop to my knees. Her soft hands tangle through my hair and she arches when I give a long slow pass with my tongue. I linger at her chest, pretty sure I've found heaven.

"Yes, just like that," she murmurs.

I turn my attention to the other nipple, and knead her breasts, grazing her with my teeth and squeezing a little harder than I normally would, but fuck . . . Heat builds in the room and I feel like I'm sixteen again, jacked up on testosterone.

I grab my pants, and pull out a condom. I toss it onto the bed as I give her a little shove. She falls back, and I nearly lose my shit then and there when she widens her legs in sweet invitation. I stand there for a moment, trying to remember how to breathe.

Tonight sweet Summer is all mine. Finally.

I rip into the foil with my teeth and quickly sheathe myself. I slide onto the bed, and grip her thighs. I squeeze hard enough to leave a bruise as I widen them even more, my gaze going to her wet pink pussy. I drop down on her, pressing her into the mattress with all my weight, restraining her beneath me.

Her legs lift, wrap around me, squeeze my waist, and I reposition myself between her thighs. I push her damp hair from her face. "I'm going to fuck you like this the first time so I can watch you come. But next time, I'm going to flip you over, tie your hands to that bedpost, and do whatever I want to you." I stare at her for a moment, watch her mouth open and close. "Just wanted to let you know."

"Okay," she whimpers, but the heat in her eyes tells me it's from excitement not fear.

I look between our bodies. "I want you to take all of me, every inch." I have no idea why I'm asking that of her. I only ever needed a few inches inside to get off. But for some unknown reason I needed to be buried in her, balls fucking deep. I press my palms to her bent knees, and position my cock at her sweet opening. I meet her eyes waiting for an answer.

"Yes," she whispers, and then I don't hear anything else. I drive into her, pounding into her sweet pussy with a ferocious-ness that slams the headboard against the wall. Her nails scratch at my back, and I ride her. She's so tight and hot, I summon every ounce of control I possess to hang on. Her hips rise up to meet my thrusts, and I pump a few more times before I shift to watch my cock slide in and out. Man, that's so hot.

Feeling a little out of control, I press a finger to her clit, and she whimpers. "I need to get deeper. Tell me you can take me deeper?"

"Yes."

I power my hips forward and work my cock inside, giving her more inches than I've ever given anyone. I expected resistance, and I am careful not to hurt her, but her body opens for me, taking me in, swallowing me whole.

Un-fucking-believable.

Once I'm all the way in I still, and capture her mouth. Her pussy clenches around me, holds me tight and I groan. Jesus everything about her feels so good. I devour her sensual mouth, suck her bottom lip. Her hands rake over me with aroused eagerness and she moves her hips, wanting more.

I pull almost all the way out and piston back into her. She gasps, and I repeat the motion. It's insane how good it feels. She whimpers as I fuck her, and it reduces me to a mass of quivering need. Pleasure races, takes hold, controls. Makes me fucking mad. Restraint a thing of the past, I ram. Heavy thrust. Rough. She moans with every surge.

She breathes unevenly against my neck. I inch back to see her but she looks gone, lost in ecstasy. I fucking love this look on her. A lot. Too much.

I place trembling arms on either side of her head, my blood pulsing hot, burning me from the inside out. I come down hard, my pubic bone stroking her clit, and her pussy squeezes, followed by a hot flow of release. Her breath becomes jagged as she cries out. *Fuck yes.* With my body thrumming, entirely lost in the moment—in Summer—I pump furiously, refusing to give in to the sensation. But when her pussy tightens around my entire length, her hot heat frying my last working brain cell, I shudder in surrender and let go. I pulse inside her, throb with an intensity unlike ever before. Christ.

I fall down next to her and she moans when I pull her to me. My heart crashes as I gather her into my arms. She rests her head against my chest, her other hand flattens on my stomach. As she touches me, I kind of want to ask her to stay for breakfast, spend the afternoon, go for a motorcycle ride, and quilt a fucking blanket. Christ almighty. What the fuck is going on? Eyes closed she shifts, and puts her head on my shoulder. Her breath is hot on my neck.

"Sean," she whispers against my temple, her breathing changing, becoming even.

I watch her as she sleeps, and fight my own exhaustion, desperate to stay awake so I can take her again. I shut my eyes for a brief second, and when I open them again, a hint of light is glinting in through the crack in the curtains. I hear movement at the foot of the bed, and glance up to see Summer tiptoeing to the door, shoes in hand. Her long dark hair, mussed from sex and sleep, falls over her back, and I want to tug it again, to pin her beneath me and force her mouth to mine. My heart speeds up and I can't let her go. Not yet.

"Your hair," I say, my voice rough and scratchy from arousal.

"What?" She turns back and I glance at her over the blankets.

"It's so different."

Her face pales, a flash of unease passes through her gaze. "From what?"

I stare at her. What does she mean "from what"? After last night, is she still seriously pretending not to know me, to deny that there's a little something more going on here?

"You know. From when we were kids."

She goes still. Too still. I push down on my elbows and lever myself up, but she holds her hand out to stop me. "I think you might have me confused me with someone else," she says. "We don't know each other."

What the fuck? This is Summer Wheeler, and she damn well knows who I am, too. She whispered my name for fuck's sake. I'm about to tell her that we're way past anonymity when she turns and dashes out the door. I make a move to go after her but then stop myself. Shit, any girl who straight up lies about her identity, and pretends not to know me after moaning my name can bring me nothing but trouble, and since trouble is something I'm trying to avoid right now, it's best I let her go.

Guess it's a good thing I won't be laying eyes on her again.

3

SUMMER

Even though we left Blue Bay under sad circumstances, old happy memories bombard me as I drive through town, take in the quaint, whimsically painted blue, green, purple, and red houses, the manicured lawns, and flowers growing from pots on the windowsills.

Not much had changed since I've last been here thirteen long years ago. No big box stores, no shopping malls, no chain restaurants. Everything is still small and quaint, and totally well kept. I can't help but wonder if the cottage would still be standing, having been abandoned and left neglected for over a decade. My heart gives a little start. If it isn't livable, what will I do, where will I turn? I breathe and force myself to stop thinking the worst or get ahead of myself. I can only deal with one roadblock at a time.

I turn, and take a left on Main Street, heading down the long stretch of hill toward the water. Gorgeous, trailing purple petunias spill over the mossy pots hanging from the streetlights. Such a small-town thing to do, and a welcoming sight for tourists, summer vacationers, and celebrities alike who all flock to Blue Bay to soak in the summer charm—or to hide from those wanting to . . . *apply pressure.*

The permanent knot in my stomach tightens, as I take in the beautiful town straight out of a Norman Rockwell painting—the tourist season in full swing this late in the summer. Why would Sean put this seaside town—one that his young punk ass had ruled—in his rearview mirror? I briefly pinch my eyes shut. I don't want to be thinking about Sean, or the things he did to me in his bed last night. But I can't seem to stop myself. For the first time in a long time, I'd felt safe, and my body still burns in all the hidden places he touched. I press a finger to my tingling lips, bruised and beautifully abused by his demanding mouth, and can only hope I'd been able to convince him I wasn't Summer Wheeler. Then again, if I hadn't, I'm not going to worry too much about it. From the magazine articles and spotlights done on America's favorite motocross racer, he has no plans to return to Blue Bay—ever.

Thank God.

Still, I wonder what drove him away. I pass Benny's grocery store, and my heart squeezes in my too tight chest as memories continue to filter in. Laughter catches my attention and I turn to see a group of teens hanging around outside Sugar's, the town's one and only ice cream shop. Everywhere I look, everything I see reminds me of my mother, of happier days.

Every Saturday we'd hike up the hill from our cottage, order our groceries for the week, then go for ice cream before they were delivered to our door. Shopping and going to Sugar's was one of my favorite things to do with my mom. My dad was away at sea a lot, and many summers it was just my mom and me. We were close, and the pain of her loss still crashes over me like a powerful tsunami wave.

On numerous trips to town we'd see Sean racing through

the streets on his motorbike, Officer Walker tight on his heels. A smile pulls at me, even though I'm not supposed to be thinking of him. I would lick my ice cream cone, and feign disgust, mimicking my mother's reaction, but secretly my heart was wobbling, rooting for the bad boy I'd been warned to stay away from.

As I approach the water, I roll my window down. I taste the salty brine on my tongue, savor the sweet memories it pulls from the dark corners of my mind. I breathe it in and a sound catches in my throat. I'm a long way from home, where the air is thick and car horns, rather than crashing waves, lull me to sleep at night.

I slow when I see our cottage tucked between two gorgeous mansions. My place is battered and worn from the salty ocean, curdled among the cream of the crop. I wince, surprised that the town council hasn't bulldozed the eyesore by now. My tires crunch on the gravel as I gingerly pull up into the driveway, ready to stir the cottage awake, rip off the bandage and let old wounds weep.

The roar of the truck's hemi dies down as I kill the engine, and I sit still for a moment, breathing past the harder childhood flashbacks that bite like the crisp evening air after a thunderstorm. In the distance, at the back of the house, kids play in the ocean, scooping up buckets of water for their castles. A seagull soars overhead, squawking as it flaps long black-tipped wings, and the sound prompts me into action. I open the lockbox on the seat beside me and examine the two keys. One is labeled "Cottage," the other I have no idea what it's for. Does it hold clues to my father's death, my ex's betrayal? I can only hope so. I push it into my back pocket, and climb from the big cab. My feet hit the ground and as reality hits—I'm actually back in Blue Bay—I steal a glance around. I might own this place, have every right to be here, but somehow feel like an intruder, like I no longer belong.

Where do I belong?

Emptiness assaults me. I'm alone in the world and honestly don't know anymore, but that's a problem for later. Right now I need to figure out how to survive, while maintaining a low profile. I shade the late day sun from my eyes and peruse the weather-beaten cottage. A shutter hangs lopsided from the window frame, the oil-deprived hinges moaning like a wounded animal in the sea breeze. Looks like the first thing on my agenda is to make the place livable.

The front of the house faces the road, but tall shrubs and trees line the perimeter, and sides, and provide privacy. I remember planting them with my mom so long ago. I make my way to the front door and examine the exterior. My heart hitches. Such a bittersweet reunion. I continue my inspection, and step back to see the roof. It looks worn and faded, and I pray there hasn't been any water damage inside. White paint chips, discolored from the summer sun, have fallen like snow and speckle the sunburnt evergreen bushes on either side of the front door. I run my fingers over the chipped and worn railing as I take the three steps to the landing, and more flakes come off in my palm. I can take care of the cosmetic repairs myself—a splash of paint, a soapy sponge here and there—but will have to hire a local company to replace the roof, and fix whatever other damage I find inside. I have the inheritance money from Dad's will, but I don't dare touch it. Jack could probably track me if I did. Luckily he knows nothing about this place. It wasn't something Dad or I ever discussed with anyone.

But now that I'm here, I'll have to get job, one where I won't draw attention to myself. I've bussed tables before, for a little extra spending money in college, and if I have to, I'll do it again. It's not like Jenna Garridy—the name on my fake identification—can hang up a sign for chiropractor services. Someone would surely want to see her credentials.

I can only assume Dad gave me the alias because I had a friend named Jenna Garridy, and on occasion, when we were preteens, she'd accompany me to the cottage. We recently connected on Facebook, and I came to find out she's a museum curator, so it's best I go with that. I don't want to get caught up in my lies. But I'll have to come up with a story as to why I'm—or rather Jenna—is back in town, living in the Wheeler cottage.

I shove the key into the lock and wiggle it until it clicks. The scent of musk and neglect punches me in the face, and I turn my head against the assault as I wave the front door to help dissipate it. I step inside, and reach for the light. It flickers on, and I give a silent prayer of thanks that Dad kept the place powered. Maybe the light is a sign of brighter things to come. I can only hope.

The first thing I need to do is open the window and air the place out. I hurry around the cottage and crack all the windows, except for a few that have frozen shut from abandonment. A breeze cuts through from the back of the house, which overlooks the ocean, to the front.

I open the fridge, and find a case of soda, a couple missing, as well as a carton of milk, months outdated. I freeze. Had someone been here? A tingle goes down my spine as I spin—expecting to see my ex ready to pounce—but there is no one behind me.

He doesn't know where you are.

I swallow my fear, summon my bravado, and grab a soda. Maybe it was just the local teens, sneaking into the place to party, or . . . something else. Either way, no one is here now, nothing seems to be missing, and I'm thirsty. I crack the top, and take a long swallow as I check the cupboards. Empty. I walk through the place, keeping an eye out for the ledger Jack is after, or some box or locker the extra key might open. Although I don't expect it to be in plain sight if it's so important, and I'm still not convinced Dad had been here. I stumble when my shoes catch on something. I glance down. The oak floor is twisted in spots, boards turned up at the edges from years of water damage. Damn. As the costs begin to add up, and my budget bubbles over, I check the toilets and taps, and remove the sheets from the furniture. Dust catches in the light streaming in through the open windows, and I press my nose to the crook of my arm to hold back a sneeze.

I pad quietly down the hall and enter my old room. A lump punches into my throat. It's just as I remembered it, purple bedding and all. I walk around the space, touch all my old things, the stuffed toys on my pillows, old and sad as they wait for the young girl to return. But I'm no longer that young girl, innocent and loved, full of life and happiness.

I turn, and close the door on my bedroom and childhood. I stand outside my parents' room, but don't dare enter. I'm afraid to. Last time I entered the master suite, I found my mother facedown on her bed. Dead. I fight back tears as I walk into the spare room. This is where I'll be staying. I step up to the headboard, and pull the blankets down to check the mattress. It's lumpy and old and needs to be replaced.

Cha-ching.

My stomach takes that moment to grumble and I make my way back to the kitchen, abandoning my trip down memory lane. I grab my purse and toss it over my shoulder. Time to head back to town for supplies and find the name of a reputable construction company.

I leave the windows open. Since there is nothing to steal, besides ancient furniture and nostalgia, I don't bother closing the place up tight again. I climb into the driver's seat and back out of the driveway. I'd love to trade in the beast of a vehicle for something smaller, but it was my dad's and the papers are still in my father's name so I'd have a hard time proving I hadn't stolen it since my name is now Jenna. Wouldn't that be a lovely way to draw unwanted attention?

I retrace my route and find a metered spot outside the post office—an honest to God, old-fashioned post office. Town ordinance has kept this place free from large retail chains. I wouldn't much care, except I really could use a Starbucks right about now. I feed the meter, and keep my head down as I make my way to Benny's. I enter and nearly drop when I see Mr. Benny Monroe behind the counter. I can't believe he's still working. I can't believe he's still alive.

As the scent of freshly baked apple pie wafts before my nose, his gaze lifts, and when cloudy blue eyes flickers to mine I suck in air and hold it. He can't recognize me. He just can't. Save for the freckles, I'm a stark contrast to that carefree little girl. I quickly pull myself together and grab a shopping cart. The place isn't big, but it stocks everything a summer vacationer would need. The stupid front wheel on my cart wobbles as I make my way along the too narrow aisles, smiling politely at those I pass. I fill my cart, making sure to leave space for a bottle of wine or two.

Mr. Monroe keeps an eye on me, like he's trying to place me as I make my way to the cashier. I put my milk, bread, and supplies on the counter, and he rings me up with an old-fashioned register straight out of the mid-twentieth century. I feel like I'm in some sort of time warp.

"Getting a late start for the summer season, aren't you?" he asks.

I give a casual shrug. "Better late than never." His all-knowing eyes meet mine and I try not to fidget. *Don't fidget, Summer. Don't Fidget.* I fidget. *Shit.* "I'm uh . . . I bought the old Wheeler home."

Loaf of bread halfway to the paper bag, his gnarled and twisted arthritic hand stills and he angles his head. "You *bought* it."

Why did he emphasize "bought"? Did he know? "Yeah, I'm a friend of the family. Maybe you remember me. I used to come here with Summer Wheeler."

"Is that right?"

I nod. "Jenna Garridy," I say, trying the name out on my tongue. "I was talking to Summer recently and she decided to sell the place. I used to love coming here with her so much, I jumped on the chance to purchase it." *Stop rambling, Summer.* "This town, it's so quaint, and everyone is so friendly, at least that how I used to remember it."

"Still is that way," he says.

"It's totally kept the small-town feel. I just love it here."

He nods, but sorrow ghosts his eyes. "Sad thing that happened to Mrs. Wheeler. She was a nice lady."

"Yes, it was sad," I say past the tightness in my throat. Cancer. Jesus, we didn't even know Mom had a brain tumor and the next thing we know, it had taken her life. No time to prepare or say goodbye, but some people say with cancer, it's better that way.

"They were a good family. Haven't seen little Summer in years. Her father, however."

"He was back?" I ask a little too quickly, my mind going to the bottles of soda and milk. "I mean, I thought the place had been abandoned for years."

"Well, now, let's see. Summer," he says and looks me square in the eyes, "she left here close to thirteen years ago, I'd say. Her father . . . oh, let's see, Colin was by last fall."

My heart skips a beat. Dad really was here, in Blue Bay? Then maybe there is a possibility that the ledger is here somewhere. Benny studies me, like he's waiting for a reaction.

"Oh, he must have come by to get the place ready to sell," I say, proud of myself for pulling off another reasonable response when my insides are in chaos.

"He was a good man, too. Sad thing about his motorcycle accident."

"Yes, a horrible accident," I say, but after overhearing my ex on the phone, I'm not so sure it was an accident. I study Benny and wonder how he'd heard the news of my dad. He might be old but obviously nothing gets by him. I make a mental note to be extra careful and chose my words wisely around him.

He looks off into the distance, then a smile pulls at him as he continues ringing me in. "Happy to see the place is going to get used again. Such a nice property going to waste."

"Speaking of that, you wouldn't happen to know where I could find a trustworthy construction company would you?"

"Sure do." He walks over to a wall where notices and business cards populate a corked board. He removes a card and hands it to me. "Best in the business, as long as you don't mind a little cussing. The Blue Bay crew isn't known for their church going ways. If you know what I mean."

I smile and glance at the card. Nothing fancy just, "Blue Bay Construction" and a phone number and address on it.

"They'll do right by you, missy."

"Thanks, I'll check them out."

I hand over a hundred-dollar bill—not wise to use my credit card—pocket the pennies in change, and gather up my two brown bags.

"I hear they're all coming back to town," Mr. Monroe says, a hint of melancholy in his voice. "Their father was a great man who'd give you the shirt off his back if you needed it, but he was damn hard on those boys, always on them about something. But he just wanted to raise hardworking, respectable sons." He pauses for a moment. "Some say he was too hard, especially after they lost their mother, but they were good kids, though." He chuckles and adds, "Underneath it all."

I think Mr. Monroe might be losing it. "Excuse me?" I say, having no idea what he's talking about.

"The boys. They're all coming back. At least that's the rumor."

"Who?"

The bell over the door jingles, and the old man's face lights up. "Well wouldn't you know it. Here's one of them now."

I spin, and the edges of my vision fade, until I see only him. Tall, powerful, mouthwateringly sexy. The poster boy for bad intentions and all kinds of wrong for me—no matter how good the sex was, or how many times he lit me up like it was the damn Fourth of July.

"I . . . you . . ." I stumble over my words, my rattled brain trying to catch up. Sean is here. In the flesh.

Oh. My. God.

His gorgeous green eyes darken when they meet mine, then slide to my mouth, fixate on it. He stiffens, his gaze jerking back to mine, and I'm impressed at how quickly he recovers from the shock of seeing me. Much quicker than me, unfortunately.

"Hey," he says.

"Hey yourself," I manage to get out.

He gives a slight smile and his dimple flirts with his cheek, ridiculously sexy. "You're back."

"I'm . . . staying here for a while, yes. I had no idea I'd see you here in Blue Bay."

"I live here."

I shrug and say, "I had no idea. I'd vacationed here a time or two, but I'm sorry, I have no memory of you."

A pause and then, "Jesus Christ." He rakes agitated fingers though his hair, and glares at me, a scowl on his face. "What the fuck are you doing?" he asks in a voice that is low, too low. And too dangerous.

I shuffle the bags in my hands as a flock of birds take flight in my stomach. "Just getting my groceries."

"Summer, it's me, Sean," he says through gritted teeth. "Tell me what's going on."

I'm wound so tight, my motions are robotic as I set my bags down and pull my fake identification from my purse. Self-preservation warns me to run, as far away from this town —Sean—as I can. If only I had somewhere else to hide to, I would. After Mom's death, Dad and I moved around a lot with his work, two lost souls with nowhere to really call home. I never made many friends because of it and have none that I can run to now.

I flash him my fake identification. "See."

He rubs the back of his neck. "Yeah, okay." He's conceding but his voice remains dubious. "Whatever you say, *Jenna Garridy.*" Another pause and then, "So this friend you're meeting, she lives here?"

"Yeah, it's Summer Wheeler. I'm buying the old cottage. She was going to meet me here, but she's tied up at work and can't make it back after all. I think you're mixing the two of us up."

He studies me, his expression cautious, dark. Threatening. The muscles along his jaw tick and he looks behind him, like he's trying to decide whether to get the hell out of Dodge or invest in my story.

He turns back to me, his gaze raking over my face with intimate recognition. I stand there, my brain buzzing like a fine wine. Do I mention last night or not? Since it was my first one-night stand I'm not versed in morning-after proto-col. Deciding it best not to bring it up and forget it ever happened, I say, "If you'll excuse me," I show him the Blue Bay Construction card. "I need to find the man who runs this company and see about a few repairs to my cottage."

His hand closes over my wrist, not tight, but firm enough

to hold me still. It brings back heated images from last night, and the way he held me down, used and abused me so thoroughly. My legs wobble as my body comes to life under his touch and it's all I can do not to confess, tell this man who makes me feel so safe—yet is a danger to me in so many ways—the whole truth, including how much I want him again. Then again the way my nipples are poking against my shirt is confession enough.

"You found him," he says, his teeth still clenched.

"What? Found who?"

"The man in charge. You found him," he says, his voice as dark and deep as the Atlantic waters hugging Blue Bay's coastline.

My toes curl.

Last night, he was definitely the man in charge—of my entire body. I breathe deep and the faint hint of soap and open road wash over me. I revel in it, my body shuddering with awareness.

"I didn't realize." I shove the card into my purse. "I'll find someone else in town."

"Why would you do that?" he asks, his voice like a rough caress that I feel all the way to the needy spot between my legs.

I take in his hard eyes, the way they're burning into me. "You look like you want me to."

He tears his gaze away, and glances out the glass door again, but his thumb continues to brush my hand, a slow, steady sweep over my flesh that is doing the most ridiculous things to my body. Does he even know he's doing that?

His gaze is murderous when he turns back to me. "It's like this, my competition are going to see you coming a country mile away."

I pull my hand back. God, if he keeps touching me like

that, I'm going to drop my panties for him again. "What's that supposed to mean?" I spit out.

"A single girl. A Blue Bay cottage in need of repair. Old money." He rubs the rough pads of his thumb and forefinger together, and I stop breathing, not wanting to remember how I know those big fingers of his are rough. "They'll eat you alive."

"I'm on a bit of a tight budget so—"

"Which is why you're going to hire me." He steps into me, crowding me, so big and strong and tough, his presence edgy but comforting. I fight the urge to snuggle into him, hand myself over and beg him to make me forget again—just for a few more hours.

"You won't . . . eat me alive?" What the hell am I doing? He's not a guy I should tease or tempt. Last night was a one-night shot, and I don't need the complications of Sean, the way I had so easily lost myself in him. If I want to survive I need to keep all my wits about me, and trust no one.

He grins, that sexy dimple stroking me in places so deep, it physically pains me not to lie down and spread for him. "Not unless you want me to."

SEAN

Okay, this confirms it.

I'm a masochist. A goddamn motherfucking masochist.

Not unless you want me to.

Why the fuck would I say that?

Yeah, okay so I momentarily forgot I was back in Blue Bay, walking the straight and narrow, and this girl has trouble written all over her. I should stay away from Summer Wheeler—or rather Jenna Garridy—if that's who she's pretending to be.

Jenna Garridy, the kid who'd accompanied Summer here a time or two. No way am I getting them mixed up, which begs the question: why is Summer lying to me?

Does she think for one minute that I'd forgotten about the time I pulled her from the water, gave her mouth-to-mouth down by the shore? Her lips were so firm and sweet: spun candy, sugar, and honey all wrapped up into one tasty package. After that incident, she followed me around, and I dodged her at every turn. But fuck, no way could I ever forget about the girl who starred in my first wet dream—and continues to star in them today.

I breathe in her floral scent, take in her freshly scrubbed face, free of makeup, as she squares her shoulders, trying to pull off tough girl. But the act is wasted on me. I know who she really is, and I know underneath her put together appearance and bravado, she's quaking like a goddamn leaf in a windstorm.

Unable to help myself I sway closer, my body reliving last night. I'd been a little rough, a little greedy with her, but having her in my bed was far too many years in the making. The noises she made, Jesus, they're still buzzing through my brain, chugging along like a freight train and stirring the need inside me. The moans, the sexy little whimpers, and the way her mouth opened but no sound came when she climaxed.

Fucking perfect.

As my dick swells, she lifts her chin. "If you want to stop by in an hour or so to give me an estimate on the damages, I'd appreciate it."

My gaze drops to the mouth I ache to ravage again, to lips that are still swollen from my hard kisses. She's even more beautiful in the afternoon sun, her pretty features no longer masked in the dim light of a grimy hotel. She gathers her bag and makes her way to the door.

"Yeah, sure," I say, and stare at her jean-clad backside as she exits the store, drops her groceries into the back of her big ass truck, and makes her way across the street to Sugar's. I give myself a lecture. *Run the other way, dude*. But I can't seem to tear my gaze away. Since we've already established that I'm a masochist, I step outside and wait for her to emerge so I can watch her lick that ice cream cone the same way I want her to lick my cock.

Motherfucker.

I shove my hands into my pockets, anything to prevent me from whipping out my dick and stroking it. Fuck, why the hell did I agree to work on her place? By rights I should ask one of my brothers, or one of my cousins. I'd do just that, except I'm the only Owens boy who's made it home so far. Soon enough the guys will all trickle in, just not soon enough for me.

I pace and wipe the moisture from my brow as I bake in the hot afternoon sun. Why did I push for the job?

Because this is Summer Wheeler and she's walking around with a goddamn lost look on her face. I might be a lot of things, but I'm not a guy to turn his back on girl who's running—from someone or something.

A few people on the streets pass by me, slowing as recognition hits. I nod, and a couple nod back. Most don't. Guess they're not too happy to see one of the problematic Owens boys back in town. But they don't need to worry. I have no intentions of causing trouble, even though it seems to have found me in the name of Summer.

Or rather Jenna.

Speaking of *Jenna,* she exits the ice cream shop, and her steps slow to a crawl when she finds me watching. I lean against the brick building and cross my legs, in no hurry to go anywhere. I stare. Transfixed. She pulls her gaze away and scurries down the street, to disappear into one of the boutiques. I want to go after her, demand she tell me what the fuck is going on, but every muscle in my body tenses when a black-and-white pulls up to the curb in front of me.

Fuck. Just what I need. I've been in town all of a few hours and I'm already getting hassled by the cops. I push off the wall and straighten to my full height.

"Walker," I say, as he climbs from the driver's seat. In the ten years I've been gone he hadn't changed much, just a little rounder around the gut, but still as mean and spiteful as a hairpin turn on a rainy fucking day.

"Sean." He saunters around his car, his right hand on his hip, near his gun, a gesture meant to intimidate, I suppose. Some would say I have a death wish when out on the open road with my bike. Maybe that's true, maybe it's not. Either way, it's been a long time since I've been afraid of anyone or anything. "Heard you were back in town."

"Miss me?"

He chuckles but it holds no humor. He steps up to me, invades my personal space, close enough that I can smell stale coffee and a cream puff on his breath. I want to push back, it's a primal reaction, but Grandma Nellie is waiting for her groceries and I'm not interested in finding myself locked up for the night. I have too much shit to do. Plus I'm the oldest Owens, home to put things in order and lead my brothers and cousins by becoming a model citizen.

You need to set an example for the others.

As my father's words ping around inside my brain, Walker's nostrils flare. "Listen, pal. Don't think for one minute I'm going to tolerate you, or any one of your fucking crew tearing up these streets. This is a nice respectable place now and I expect it to stay that way. Understand?"

"Not looking for trouble," I bite back through clenched teeth. "Just back home to take care of Dad's funeral arrangements." I don't bother to tell him that I'm actually here for good. That will be a nice surprise for later.

At the mention of my dad, he stiffens. The two have a history, which is why Walker has been riding our asses for as long as I can remember. Then again, our rivalry could have less to do with my dad stealing his girl and marrying her back in the day, and more to do with me tearing up the streets on my bike and roughing up the dickless rich boys who summered here and thought they were better than the locals from the other side of the tracks.

He tips his hat. "Yeah, sorry to hear about his passing," he says, and he looks genuinely apologetic. "Give my blessings to Grandma Nellie."

I nod and stand over him a moment longer, then his radio goes off and he backs up. I exhale slowly to get rid of my pent-up energy, but it doesn't work. In times like these I either need a good race or a hard fuck with someone I won't ever lay eyes on again. Both of which I've given up. I give another sweep of the streets before stepping back into Benny's. The fresh scent of apple pie reaches my nostrils. My olfactory senses kick in, and take me back ten years.

"Hey Benny, how have you been?" I ask, shaking off my encounter with Officer Asshole as I glance at the row of pies cooling on the rack. "I see Judy is still making her fabulous apple pies."

The old man comes out from around the corner and opens his arms. "Sean," he says. "So good to see you." He inches back and his cloudy eyes that see all look me over. "And in one piece."

"Mostly," I say, my shoulder taking that moment to pain, a reminder of the break that failed to heal properly. Probably because I'd hopped back on my bike before giving it a chance to. But I had a race to win, something to prove.

He frowns. "Sorry about your dad. He was a good man."

"Thanks." I look past his shoulder, unable to take in the deep sadness on his face. If I do, I might fucking sob.

"I see you met the new owner of the Wheeler cottage," he says, changing the subject, clearly picking up on the shit storm going on inside me. *I should have been here. Fuck, I should have been a better son.* "I heard you were all coming home, so I gave one of your dad's cards to her," he adds, his voice pulling me back.

"Thanks for that. We can use the work."

"Are you taking the job?" Benny's eyes narrow, and I get the distinct impression that he's asking something else entirely. The man is sharp, has been around for years, and I take it he, too, knows Summer is pretending to be someone else. But most probably wouldn't know her. She's changed a lot over the years.

"Yeah, I'll help her," I say, answering the question he's really asking.

He puts his hand on my shoulder. "You're a good boy, Sean."

I scratch the back of my head. "So, uh, Grandma sent me here to pick up her order."

He nods. "It's a big one. I guess she's preparing for the return of all her grandsons." He waves toward the row of brown bags piled behind the cash register.

"Looks like she's cooking for an army." Then again, I guess, in a way she is. When the Owens brothers and cousins convene, we do form an army, and impenetrable force. Fuck with one Owens, you fuck with them all. It's always been that way, and we grew even closer with our cousins, Ryan, Carter and Jace when their parents, my aunt and uncle, died in a car crash when they were young. All three moved into the old homestead with us and Dad treated them like they were his own, and yeah, he was just as hard on them, too. "Good thing I brought the truck."

Benny shuffles his way back to the counter, his leather loafers scratching against the scuffed floor. "Let me help you."

"No I got this," I say and follow him to load up the bags. I steal a glance around the mom-and-pop store. Other than the jars of candy he used to keep on the counter, not much has changed in the years I've been gone. Back in the day Benny used to slip me a candy whenever I came in. In return, I'd help him with his deliveries. I always liked the old man, but Jesus he should be retired by now.

I finish loading the last bag, and wave. "Talk to you soon, Benny. Give Judy a hug for me."

"Don't be a stranger," he says, and the bell overhead rings as I shut the door and climb into my truck. I turn the ignition over, and pass Summer's truck when I spin around in the middle of the street and head back to the old homestead.

How the hell am I going to do a walk-through of her place without wanting to put my hands all over her again? My dick throbs in anticipation, and I work to marshal it. I crack my window and suck in a breath of humid air. I really should wait until one of the guys come home and give him the job. Getting tangled up in her mess, whatever it might be, isn't conducive to walking the straight and narrow. But how the fuck am I supposed to walk away? My late mother and Grandma Nellie raised me better than that.

I drive for a few more miles and my heart squeezes when I pull into the lane leading to the big house built by my great-grandfather when Blue Bay was a whaling village, long before the tourists began flocking here. I slow my speed, and look past my motocross bike in the driveway, to the big house rising up behind it.

Dad was the best carpenter in all of Connecticut but his own place is in need of repair. A wooden swing moves in the summer breeze, and I study the front porch, the sagging roof over it. My gaze slowly moves to the room he added on when I was away.

His office.

My office now, I suppose, now that the old man is gone. Bile punches into my throat as his loss crashes over me, and a blind fist hammers my gut, fierce and punishing.

I can't believe he's gone.

Nellie steps outside and hurries to the truck, and I harden myself. I don't want her to see my pain. "Did you get my shortening?" She begins to peek into all the bags.

"I don't know. Didn't look through."

She gives me that look—the one that could scare the head

off a chicken and helped keep us boys in line after we lost our mother during our rebellious teen years. "I can't bake your favorite pie if you didn't get my shortening."

"I'm sure it's all in there, Gram."

She picks up two bags and carries them into the house. I shake my head. No matter what she's been through, she's still as tough as a tractor. I follow with an armload and she's already unloading her bags by the time I reach her. I begin to help her, but she swats at me like I'm a nuisance fly.

"Get. You know I don't like anyone fussing in the kitchen with me."

I shake my head again. Some things never change. I turn to leave her to her baking, but when I do I feel the heavy emptiness of the place. Hollow silence. Ghosts in every corner. I swallow. Maybe some things do change.

The last time I was home this house was filled with my brothers and cousins, laughing around the table, fighting on the living room floor, or helping dad with one chore or another. I cough down the lump climbing into my throat.

"I'll be in Dad's office. Have some paperwork to look over," I say, trying to inject a lightness in my voice I don't feel. But right now, if Gram turns to hug me, or console me in any sort of way, I might fucking lose it.

The screen door squeals as I push through it, and I make a mental note to oil it. The heat of the day closes around me as I make my way to Dad's office. I try the door and it's open. Of course. I walk in, and my father's presence slams through me like a physical blow. A spill on my bike followed by full-force trauma to the head would have been less painful. Grief presses down on me, heavy, suffocating, weaving its way around me and sucking the air from my lungs. I try to breathe past it when all I want to do is to lie down and curl around it, let it consume me. I squeeze my eyes shut and work to keep my shit together. When I open them again, I catalog the room. I need to go over the books, but where the hell do I start?

Files and papers are strewn everywhere. Oak bookshelves lining one wall, Dad's handiwork, overflows with balled-up permits and forms and invoices, some marked paid, others still owing. He was a carpenter, for Christ's sakes, not an accountant. Why the hell didn't he hire someone to help?

Because he was waiting for one of his boys to step up and be the man he needed them to be.

Unable to breathe, I sink into the chair. The same one he'd died in. Wide open and vulnerable, I choke back the tears burning behind my eyes, ears, and throat. I pinch my lids shut, and work diligently to refill my lungs. A rumble catches in my throat as my fingers curl around the arms of the chair and squeeze until my knuckles turn white.

I pray to fucking God he didn't suffer too much, that his life passed quickly and he didn't have time to think about his dick-ass sons who'd abandoned the Owens homestead the first chance they could. I lean forward and drop my head onto his desk. In the balled-up letter still stuffed in my back pocket, Nellie wrote that the heart attack was quick and painless, but I call bullshit. My guess is she only said that for my benefit. She always was one to protect her grandsons, especially when the old man was tearing us a new one. We never could live up to the expectations he had of us.

As betrayal eats at me, rakes my insides raw and leaves me bleeding, the office door opens. I straighten, half expecting it to be Dad, storming in to yell at me for lying down on the job. My gaze meets eyes identical to mine and I jump from my seat.

"Look what the fucking cat dragged in."

Tyler, my tough-ass baby brother, gives me a once-over. The devil's grin spreads across his pretty boy face—his innocence long gone. Much like the rest of us. "You're one to talk."

I circle the desk and step up to him. He might be the baby of the family, but he has a few inches on me. I grab his chin, turn his head from left to right. "What happened to that pretty face of yours?" I ask, rattling his cage.

"Got prettier," he says, jerking from my hold.

I smirk. "You must be punch-drunk, little brother. Looks to me like someone's mistaken your face for a punching bag."

"Don't be so jealous that I got all the looks in the family, bro."

I throw my arms around him and drag him to me. "I'm glad you're home." We hug and it feels good. Actually it feels like a long fucking time coming. "Missed you, kid."

He fists my shirt. "Don't be going and getting all senti-mental on me," he says, even though he's holding me to him instead of pushing me way. "Or I'll beat the shit out of you."

I inch back, and he pins me with a scowl, but I don't miss the moisture in his eyes. He sniffs and tries to hide it. My heart seizes as reality hits. I'd left Tyler, too. Jesus fucking Christ. I'd climb straight into hell for this kid, no questions asked, but I'd been so goddamn selfish, out for my own plea-sures, and to prove some bullshit worthiness to the world— my father—that it hadn't occurred to me that when I turned my back on Dad, I walked away from a fourteen-year-old boy who needed his big brother. I'd set an example, which is probably why he left first chance, too. Jesus, we've all been through so much, it's been away too long. It's time I do right by this family. I owe them that much and I never want to let my father down again.

I make a fist and nudge his chin. "If I didn't have so much to do, I'd meet you in the ring, and prove I'm still your big brother."

He laughs, but it doesn't reach his eyes. "We don't have

rings where I fight, brother." He looks past me, takes stock of the office, and the air grows heavier as silence beats down on us. His eyes meet mine again, and he swallows. His way of fighting off the rawness? Probably.

"When's the funeral?" he asks, addressing the big elephant in the room, one that's taking up space. Hollowing us out inside.

I walk back to Dad's desk and plunk down into his old chair. I can almost feel him in the room, looking at us with disgrace for abandoning the family, the business. But fuck man, he was a hard-ass son of a bitch. Unbearable. Intolerable. Set in his ways, and a motherfucking nightmare to work with.

I miss him so fucking much.

All I ever wanted was his approval, for him to just once tell me I was doing a good job—that he was proud of me. I suspect the same of Tyler, and every other Owens offspring. I grab a pen and tap it against the file on the desk. "He's been cremated. Those were his wishes. We'll bury him next to Mom at the cemetery as soon as everyone gets back."

He plunks himself down into the hard wooden chair across from me and swallows uneasily. "Where do we start?"

I glance around the room. "I need to go over the books and see what kind of shape the company is in. From what Grandma Nellie said, Dad hadn't been taking on too many jobs over the last few years and bills were piling up." I plan to put all the money I won on the circuit into getting the business booming again. I'll need to pay outstanding bills, have money for supplies and outlay of expenditures, as well as pay the guys. I can't expect them to work for nothing after dragging them all back here. It's going to eat up all my savings, but Ty doesn't need to know that.

"How's Grandma?"

I scoff. "Tough as ever, and in the kitchen cooking up a feast."

Ty rubs his stomach. "I miss her cooking. Hope she's making meatloaf."

I take in his muscled body. Hard as granite. Unbreakable steel. "Doesn't look like that stopped you from getting a meal," I say, implying he's gotten a little soft around the middle.

"Stop with the jealousy, bro," he teases. I laugh, and it eases the tension inside me. To look at Tyler, a tough-as-nails underground brawler, you'd never know that beneath it all he's funny, charming, soft as fuck. We all are.

"What the fuck is wrong with Walker anyway?" Tyler asks.

I stiffen. "He's riding you, too?"

He pulls something from his back pocket and slams it on the desk. "Speeding ticket."

"Bastard."

Tyler scoffs. "I was going five miles over the limit. What the fuck is still up his ass anyway?"

"Call your brothers and cousins. Warn them Walker is looking to make his mark on us and prove he runs this town."

Ty nods, and pushes his hair from his face. "Yeah, all right. I'd better go see Gram."

He stands, and turns to leave. "Ty," I say to stop him. I hadn't expected him back so soon, and now that he's here I can give him our first renovation job, the Wheeler cottage.

"Yeah." He turns back, and scrubs his hand over his chin, his knuckles beaten and tattooed, but it's his scars we can't see that worry me.

I open my mouth, but instead of putting him straight to work, I say, "Good to have you back."

Fuck me hard.

5

SUMMER

After a thorough search of the cottage—even forcing myself to enter my parents' bedroom—I'm still no closer to finding the ledger. If it's not here, then where is it? With that question pinging around inside my brain, I turn my attention to my groceries, and to Sean. My hands shake as I unload the goods, my gaze going to the driveway for the hundredth time. I'd expected Sean to show up over a half an hour ago, and I'm beginning to wonder if he changed his mind on the job. Not that I can blame him. I wasn't overly friendly at Benny's, and confused him with my fake identification. I'm beginning to think his absence is for the best. Not only was he challenging my identity, a shirtless Sean in a tool belt would be too much. A girl only has so much control right?

Maybe I could get a few quotes from the other construction companies in town, play them against each other so they don't . . . *eat me alive.*

I gulp and drop a can of soup. It hits with a thud and rolls across the floor. The sound echoes through me as my mind journeys back to the way Sean had climbed between my legs and feasted on me. My God, no man had ever been so thorough with my body, taking me to places I've never been before. Heat pools hot and low in my belly, and I hug myself. Sean Owens. Hard and solid, big and tough, and even though he was rough and dirty and deliciously naughty in the bedroom, his touch gave me a measure of comfort, made me forget I wasn't alone in this world.

A bang sounds behind me. I turn and squeal, my hand going to my chest when I find Sean looming in the doorway, his heavy gaze latched on to mine.

"I . . . I didn't hear you come in," I blurt out, my breath coming a little faster, which has nothing to do with the fright he'd just given me.

His eyes narrow, skirt around the room. "You all right?"

His presence, his size and strength overwhelm me as he closes the door behind him and takes one small step toward me. "Yeah, I'm fine," I lie as my ovaries jump around like they're doing the damn Macarena.

Get it together, Summer.

"Why so jumpy?" he asks, his voice shimmering through me, the breeze blowing in off the ocean doing little to cool me down.

I look around. "You just surprised me is all. I thought I locked the door."

I always lock the door. Well, up until today, apparently. Again, another reason to stay away from the man who can preoccupy my thoughts without even trying and has me forgetting safety measures in a time when my safety is at risk.

He angles his hard body, looks around the room. "Most people don't lock their doors in Blue Bay. We have what we call a 'welcome policy.'" He pauses to do air quotes around the words. "But I guess not being from around here, you wouldn't know that."

"You're right. In SoCal we always lock our doors."

"For the record, I did knock. You didn't answer, so I let myself in."

He steps up to me, his body towering over mine, defiance written all over him as his scent curls around me, chasing away my resolve to keep my physical distance. A delicious shiver rakes down my back, and my sex clenches. What this man can do to me with just a simple look is insane. Honey-specked green eyes move over my face, a careful assessment. Outside of the Owens boys, I'd never seen eyes quite that color before. I never knew how to describe them. Tropical forest. Marshy everglades.

The ocean floor stirred up during a storm—like the one going on inside me.

"Need help?" He looks past me, his eyes zeroing in on the bags, the soup can on the floor.

"No, the can just slipped from my hand." I bend and reach for it at the same time he does and he sucks in a sharp breath when our hands collide. His thumb brushes my flesh—that same slow sweep that messes with my ability to think with clarity.

I clear my throat. "I got it, thanks." I put the can on the counter, and the coffeemaker gurgles to a stop and beeps. Thanks God. "Coffee?" I ask.

"Sure. Black."

I pour his coffee, and add a splash of milk to mine. I take a sip and wince as the nasty chlorinated tap water disguising itself as mocha java splashes over my tongue. "What is this stuff? It tastes like dirty dishwater."

His laugh rumbles through me. "When was the last time you drank dishwater?"

"Two seconds ago," I say and hold my cup up. "What I'd do for a grande Americano."

"You're not going to find a Starbucks in Blue Bay. Closest you'll get is in Hope Falls, a good twenty-minute drive."

"Might be worth it."

He steps up to my tap, and turns it on. "Let it run for a bit. Who knows when the last time this tap had been turned on."

"Thanks." I take another sip of the coffee and shudder.

"You're still going to drink it?"

I crinkle my nose. "Desperate times and all."

"Addiction?"

"Possibly."

He takes a swig and shrugs. "Not so bad. Truthfully, I've had worse." My gaze moves to his lips as he swallows, and I'm once again reminded of the greedy, openmouthed kisses he pressed against my body, between my legs.

"You can't be serious?"

"You didn't stick around for breakfast at Dick's." He laughs. "Now that was some seriously bad coffee."

At the mention of Dick's Driving Inn and Diner, my mind instantly rushes back to all the things this man did to me in his bed. A shiver races through me, and I work to shake off the need pooling between my legs.

Stop!

Alrighty then. Time for a change in subject. I wave toward the other room. "Do you need me to show you the damage?"

"Yeah," he says his voice a little deeper than it was moment ago. "I already took a look around outside, so why don't you show me what you need done in here."

Coffee in hand, I walk into the spacious living area. He follows behind me, his biker boots heavy on the floor. He stays close and I can practically feel his warm breath on my neck. I point to the ceiling. "We have water damage."

"I noticed that as soon as I came in." He shrugs. "Might not be so bad. Could be just a shingle or two. I'll climb up and have a look." Sean glances upward to take in the damage, but I'm no longer focused on the wet marks marring the ceiling. No, now I'm focused on his hard body, hewn muscles that are coiled tight and the scorpion tattoo peeking out from the top of his T-shirt. My fingers tingle, aching to trace it again, the way I had when I was in his bed.

"This wall here though," he continues. "I'm going to have to tear it down. See how it's bulging?" Oh yeah, I can definitely see how it's bulging, except I'm not looking at the wall. He steps away from me, and runs one big hand over the bloated plasterboard.

He looks back at me but I'm far too slow to react. He catches me staring at his ass, and heat races through me, no doubt painting my cheeks pink.

I guess this is as good a time as any to address the tension between us. "Last night," I begin.

"What about it?"

"It was . . ."

He arches a brow. "Fun."

Fun? Yeah that's just one of the many words to describe the best sex of my life.

"It was a one-time thing." I look at my flats and wiggle my toes. "I don't normally—"

"I know," he says and my gaze jerks to his, to take in deeply intelligent eyes that can see right through me.

"You do?"

"Yeah, Jenna, I do. And don't worry, one-night stands are my specialty."

I flush at that, then realize he'd called me Jenna.

Good.

I work to pull myself together. "The floors," I say, needing desperately to change the direction of conversation before I tell him I'm kidding—or rather show him—by pushing my panties to my ankles and asking him to take me again. It takes everything I have not to. "They're damaged from the water as well." I look down, but he doesn't follow my gaze. I feel the weight of his stare as I kick at the damaged turned-up corners. "I'm on a tight budget and I can live with them like this. I think we should concentrate on the roof. I can do the cosmetic things myself, like paint and clean."

"Jenna."

I glance back up to find him watching me, carefully. "Yeah?"

"I'm sure I can give you a good deal, and fix your floors under budget, too."

"Okay," I say for lack of anything else. "I have to run to town for a few more things. Should I just leave you here to get started?" He holds his hand out, and my heart thumps wildly, the chemistry between us beating like ceremonial drums, going louder and louder in my ears. I stare at his open hand. Is he waiting for me to slide mine in his so he can take us to the bedroom?

"Key," he finally says.

"Right." I run to the kitchen to grab my purse, happy for the reprieve. "When I was in town I had few extra made. I'm known for misplacing my keys all the time."

I hand him one, and he shoves it into his front pocket, the action tugging his jeans lower.

"What about the bedrooms?" he asks.

"What about them?"

His mouth twitches, presenting that sexy dimple. "Any damage?"

"Ah, no, just need to be aired out."

"Mind if I look?"

"No, go ahead."

I don't follow him—after searching them earlier, I'm not anxious to enter again—instead I say, "I'll leave you to it. I'm heading out and will be a few hours." I leave him to his work and jump back in my truck. If I'm going to sleep here for the rest of the summer, I'm going to need to order a new mattress and fresh bedding. I pull from the driveway, and glance at the ocean in my rearview mirror.

I head back to town, and think about the key in my back pocket. I'll have to look around, see what it might open. What I don't want to do is run around and start checking every lock like a crazy woman. That will only draw unwanted attention to me. Sean doesn't seem to trust the local sheriff as it is, so I don't want him questioning my actions.

As I drive past the local pub, Winchesters, and see a HELP WANTED sign, I slow. This late in the summer most of the local students are likely heading back to college soon. Just my luck. I park my truck and steal a glance around, still a bit jumpy and worried that Jack has tracked me. When my gaze comes up empty, I try to present calm and make my way inside.

I give my eyes a moment to adjust to the dimmer light and catalog the room before making my way toward the bar. The dinner crowd hasn't filed in yet, so the place is fairly quiet, just a couple guys sitting on stools across from the bartender—one of them a big scary dude full of tattoos—and a group of girls around my age, lingering at a table as the wait-ress serves them fresh margaritas. I catch a hint of their conversation as I pass. They're talking about some new guy in town, and taking bets on who'll get to sleep with him first. I can't help but wonder if they're talking about Sean. A flash of possession ties my stomach in knots as I step up to the bar. What the hell? Sean isn't mine. He can date any one of these girls. I hope he does, actually. That way I can stop thinking about him and concentrate on why I'm really here. I lift my finger and gesture to the guy behind the counter. He nods and makes his way to me.

With a quick flick, he tosses a rag over his shoulder. "What can I get for you?"

"Actually, I'm here to apply for a job."

He points to the manager's office. "Right over there."

"Thanks." I push off my stool, and peruse the establishment a second time. It's old, in need of refurbishment, but it's clean and the waitresses don't have to wear shirts that show off their boobs. Anything is a step up from Dick's Driving Inn and Diner though, right? I make my way to the manager's office and find the door cracked. I knock, and the man behind the counter perks up.

"Come in."

I plaster on my best smile, and enter. The guy behind the desk doesn't look much older than me. I wonder if I knew him back in the day. "I'm Jenna Garridy," I say. "I see that you're hiring."

He holds his hand out. "James Beckman. Everyone calls me Beck."

His name doesn't ring a bell, which is good. I don't want anyone remembering me. I'm risking enough with Sean as it is. Why again am I doing that? Because he's giving me a good deal on renovations? Or is it because being around him makes me feel safe, even though it shouldn't? "Nice to meet you, Beck."

The wheels on his chair squeal as he pushes away from his desk. In typical guy fashion, he folds one leg over the other, resting his foot on his knee. "You have experience?"

I nod. "Plenty. I waitressed my way through college."

"College?" His eyes narrow and he rubs his chin. "You think maybe you're a little too qualified?"

"I'm a museum curator. Lost my job, recently moved here," I say quickly before I blow this. "I'm a hard worker, and I won't let you down."

"Things slow at the end of the summer. Hours will be cut, you okay with that?"

"Yes, that's fine." I say. "Bought the old Wheeler house,

fixing it up and probably won't be here much past the summer season." At least I hope not. I have a job in SoCal to get back to, once I figure out what it is my ex is after.

He opens his mouth to respond, but a noise at the door stops him. I turn and meet with familiar green eyes. My breath catches for a moment at the gorgeous sight.

"Hey, Beck. I'm taking off. Big brother is calling. Looks like he's got a job for me already." The man, a younger, more tattooed version of Sean, stops talking for a minute, and his gaze moves to mine, lingers a bit, then blatantly checks me out. His smile is that of the devil's himself when he grins and turns back to Beck.

"Tyler, meet Jenna. She's applying for the waitress position."

"Jenna," Tyler says, zeroing back in on me, my mouth specifically. The Owens boys seem to have a fixation with lips. "Nice to meet you," he says in a sexy, lazy way that undoubtedly has women shedding their panties. He's big, tough, and gorgeous, but he's no Sean, at least not to me.

"Nice to meet you, too, Tyler."

He flashes that bad boy grin again. "Talk soon," he says, his eyes still on me.

"Later," Beck says.

Tyler leaves and I turn back to Beck, my hands folded on my lap. "As I was saying, I bought the old Wheeler cottage. I even hired Sean Owens to work on it." Why am I bringing Sean's name into the conversation? Name-dropping because Beck is a friend of his brother? Or maybe I just want to hear it on my lips?

Jesus, Sean isn't even here and he's still messing with me.

"Already?"

"What?" I ask, dragging my mind back to the conversation.

"He just got in to town today, I didn't expect he'd start working right away."

I just nod, not about to tell him I know he'd just arrived in town because we had a "thing" at a sleazy motel last night. "Why not?"

"His dad just died, which is why he's home." He shakes his head, licks his finger and wipes something off the toe of his shoe. "I thought he'd at least take a day to mourn, but I guess we all grieve in different ways, and he's got big shoes to fill, a lot of responsibility dropped on him." He frowns, and looks back at me. "Anyway, about the job."

"My hours are flexible and I promise if you hire me you won't regret it."

He goes quiet for a moment, then slides a piece of paper across his desk. "A friend of Sean's is a friend of mine. The job is yours. Can you start Monday?"

"Yes. Monday is perfect."

"Bring the papers back with you, and check with Stacey on your way out. She'll set you up with a T-shirt and apron."

"Thank you," I say, and stand to shake his hand.

I check in with Stacey then make my way outside with a shirt and apron in hand. The warm air falls over me as I weave my way around the vehicles in the lot. Totally pleased with getting a job so fast, I decide to treat myself to a few new pieces of clothing, one being a bathing suit—a full piece, of course. I don't want to do or wear anything to give Sean the impression that I want him again. I don't. Well, I do, but I'm not going to do anything about it, no matter how delicious and tempting that sounds. I have to figure out my life, what Jack is after.

Jack.

God, why did I ever get mixed up with a man under my dad's command? Oh, probably because he'd been so sweet and caring at the funeral, holding me close when I cried, and helping me take care of the arrangements beforehand. He and dad were close. I'd often heard Dad refer to him as the son he'd never had. Although in the end, there seemed to be some tension between them, but I never asked why. It wasn't my business and I assume it was work related. But all that time Jack and I were together he hadn't really been showing affection. He was getting close to me because he was after a damn ledger. So far I'm not seeing any signs of it. But if Dad had been here recently, and had given me lockbox with a key to the cottage, he must have been directing me here? Maybe I should have just gone to the police instead of running, although I had no proof other than overhearing the threat and no idea what ledger he was talking about. Once I find it, then things will be different. But at that point in time I ran, because fear makes people do crazy things.

Like sleep with old crushes.

I just hope when I get back home Sean isn't there. Our two meetings today have already overloaded my senses, and if he's hanging around in a tool belt, I might implode from want. My body warms at the image, but no way, no how am I going to fall in bed with him again.

I don't think.

6

SEAN

From my aerial view on the roof, I see Summer coming down the main road, something in the back of her truck. It's been five long days since I've started work on the house—Unfortunately her entire roof is in need of replacement—and I still can't get used to calling Summer by a fake name. Nor can I ignore the heat arching between us. When not working at Winchesters, she's been running around town like she's in search of something. Of what I don't know. When she's here, she's in short shorts and tank tops, washing the place down and scraping paint off the front porch, making it hard for me to concentrate on anything but getting my dick inside her again.

The big engine revs, announcing her arrival. Even if I hadn't spotted her I would have heard her coming a mile away. I stand, my boots thumping as I walk to the edge to see her. Like my dick hasn't been tortured enough today, right? I spot a mattress in the back of her truck, and I climb down the ladder, ready to carry it inside for her. Only problem is, a new mattress, Jenna alone in her bedroom—I see all kinds of trouble with that scenario.

I hit the last rung, and a loud *oomph* cuts through the quiet of the day. I turn, and when I see her struggling to get it off the back of the truck, I shake my head. Why the hell didn't she have it delivered? Or ask me to pick it up.

Damn stubborn woman.

I hook my thumbs into my tool belt. "What are you doing?"

"I'm painting the ceiling," she shoots back. "What does it look like I'm doing?" Her gaze drops from my face to my bare chest. "And why don't you put a shirt on?"

I grin. She scowls and mumbles curses under her breath. I'm guessing the sexual tension is getting to her every bit as much as it's getting to me. Either that or she can't find whatever it is she's looking for. Then again, maybe she's desperate for a Starbucks fix. She's been doing nothing but complaining about the coffee in this town. Seriously though, if I don't fuck her soon, I'm going to do irreparable damage. Beating off every night isn't doing a goddamn thing to ease the tension coiling tight in my cock.

Scowling back, I glare at her, and shake my head at her obstinacy. It must have killed her to ask me for help with the place, seeing how she likes to do everything on her own. "Looks like you're trying to carry a big ass mattress inside, and having trouble doing it."

"Can't get anything by you, can I?" she shoots back.

"And I'm not in a shirt because it's a million fucking degrees on the roof."

Her gaze skirts to mine again, and my cock thickens as those sexy whiskey-colored eyes rake over my chest. I can almost feel the burn marks as her heat brands me. "Fine. Don't put a shirt on then."

"Need help?"

"No, I got this." She waves me away, like she can't take me

standing there for one more second. "Just go do whatever it was you were doing."

"Okay." I stand back for a second, letting the noonday sun beat down on me, and watch her struggle. If she wasn't so sexy in those frayed shorts, and a drool-worthy tank top, I'd find humor in the situation.

But I'm not laughing.

Nope, not laughing at all.

In fact, I'm sweating like a goddamn Saint Bernard in a heat wave—smack dab in the center of Death Valley.

She manages to get the mattress from the back of the truck, but then she stumbles. The mattress goes down, and she looks like a fallen angel as she spills across it. Arms and legs splayed, breathing hard, her hair in a tumbled mess—it's more than I can fucking take. Her body beckons me, and it leaves me battered and broken like a Blue Bay fishing trawler caught in a violent Atlantic storm.

"Jenna," I say, tasting her new name on my tongue and liking the flavor it leaves. With my resolve all but gone, moisture breaks out on my body, but it's not from the afternoon sun. I swallow. Hard. My throat as dry as the Sahara, scratchy as hell, but the only thing that's going to hydrate me is her. I take a tentative step toward her, and expect her to scramble backward. She made it perfectly clear that night in the hotel was a one-shot deal, but she's not moving. Oh no, she's not moving at all.

Her chest rises and falls as she breathes harder, and her legs inch open. The movement is slight but it doesn't go unnoticed by me. At that sweet invitation, I look her over, my heart thudding hard in my chest. Jesus she is so pretty. I take in her curves, the jean shorts that are in my fucking way. I need my mouth on her, my fingers inside her panties.

A rush of sexual energy hits so hard, I'm unable to fight it anymore. As need overshadows sensibility, I drop to my knees at the foot of the mattress and a small sound catches in her throat. Her gaze shoots to my hands as I take off my tool belt and toss it aside.

"I need to fuck you," I say, no games, just the straight-up truth. I brush my hand through my hair, and her gaze roams over me. She sits up, puts her warm palms on my chest, and I'm not sure if it's to push me away or pull me closer. But then she traces my scars, my tattoo, and I resist the urge to climb to the roof and scream Halle-freaking-luliah. She looks dazed, lost in thought, her eyes imbued with lust as she trails her fingers over my flesh. My muscles flex, and harden, as she reacquaints her hands with my body. My dick aches to be inside her tight pussy. It's a need, not a want.

I put my hand over hers, bring it to my mouth and brush my lips lightly over her fingers. "I need to taste you again. I need to put my mouth all over you." I'm ready to tell her more, all the dirty things I want to do with her, but her hands are on me again, in my hair, raking across my shoulders, dragging skin on my chest.

I press my mouth to hers, and she opens for me. I thrust my tongue deep into her mouth, tasting the depths of her. So fucking sweet. But it's not enough. Lust burns through my blood as I wrench my mouth from hers. I slip my hand under her tank top, the softness of her skin, the warm scent of her flesh sets off a chain reaction in my body.

With a little nudge she falls back, and her hair splays out. I take a second to look at her, admire what's mine.

Mine?

Fuck, she's not mine. We just have this sexual pull that a few more fucks will surely sate. I ignore the part of my brain that warns a few more fucks won't be enough.

"Sean," she whispers, and the sound strokes my cock. Hardens it. Turns it into fucking granite.

"Yeah?"

Her eyes open and close, her lids fluttering fast. "Please . . ." She reaches for me and I don't even think she knows what she's begging for as I fall over her, my body pressing hers into the mattress once again. I don't give a shit that we're outside, that anyone could stumble upon us. No. All I care about is tasting her, shoving my cock so deep inside, it will finally kill the obsession I can't seem to shake.

I roll to my side, run my hands over her breasts, her stomach, and push the button through the shorts that have been driving me bat-shit crazy. I don't take them off, not yet. Instead I push my hand inside, dip into her panties and roll my finger over her clit. It's a little dirtier this way, and I want to get hot and filthy with this girl, as I get my fill and get over this fixation. Greedy with need, her hips come off the mattress, her eyes glazing with hunger.

"Yes," she whispers.

I work my finger over her swelling nub, and she's so wet and hot for me my dick jumps in my jeans. "Do you have any idea how torturous these last few days have been for me?" I ask as I sink a finger into her. So slick. Sopping wet.

Evading my question she moans, "Oh, that's so good." A keening sound rises in her throat as her hips rise up to meet my thrusting finger. I fuck her hard and deep, swiping the rough tip of my index over the tight bundle of nerves inside.

"I think you do know," I say. "I think you've been walking around here in next to nothing because you needed my cock in you again, but you're too much of a good girl to ask for it." Her eyes widened with shock and denial, and she shakes her head. I grin. "Yeah, deny it all you want. I don't believe it for a second and I ought to put you over my knee for that." The hunger in her eyes grows. Well, well, looks like the good girl likes the idea of a spanking. I stab another finger inside her and she gasps. I finger fuck her a few more times, then pull out. She cries out at the loss, but it turns in to a moan of pleasure when I flip her over.

I grip her hips and lift, until her ass is in the air. Her tight shorts hug her beautiful backside and it's all I can do to breathe as I tug them down to expose her creamy flesh. I gave her a slap and she yelps.

"No more teasing," I say. "If you want me to fuck you, just ask." Another slap, followed by another keen cry. It seeps under my skin and urges me on. "I'll give you what you want." I run my hand over her ass to soothe the sting. "Got it?" When she whimpers and moves, like she's waiting for more hard slaps, I deepen my voice. "Got it?"

"Yes," she whispers, so delirious with need I'm sure she'll agree to just about anything. Maybe she'll even agree to be my girl.

Wait, what? I'm not looking for long term, especially from a girl who's lying to me. This is just sex. Plain and simple.

"Tell me," I urge.

"I got it. When I want you to fuck me all I have to do is ask."

Hearing her talk like that sends my need into outer space, to soar where the air is thin and nothing exists but time. Time that I'll need kiss every inch of her sweet body until she's flying with me. I flip her back over, take in the flush on her cheeks. I unhook my jeans, shove them to my thighs and release my cock. Her eyes widen in pleasure as I stroke myself, a long hard tug from base to crown. Precum drips from my slit, and I'm not even sure she's aware that she's licking her lips. Fuck this is going to be good.

"Look at me." Her gaze lifts. "Do you need your mouth on me as much as I need mine on you?"

"Yes," she says, her head nodding wildly. I touch her pussy, run my finger along the seam of her jean shorts. "I'm going to eat your sweet little pussy. I'm going to tongue you so deep you'll still feel my mouth on you, long after we're done. Then you're going to take my cock in your mouth, little girl. You're going to put your tongue all over me and take me deep, until you can't breathe." I push aside the scrap of material covering her hot sex, and run my finger over the crotch of her damp panties. "You're going to show me how much you want my cock in here."

I grab her shorts, tug them down her thighs until her gorgeous cunt is exposed. Heaven. Pure fucking heaven. She's wiggling, trying to get her shorts down farther, to widen her legs. But I don't let her just yet. Yeah, when I take her she'll be wide open and begging for it, but watching her squirm, and having her at my mercy like this is too fucking sexy.

I climb over her, press a knee into the matters on either side of her trapped legs and take in her groomed pussy. "Did you do this for me?" I ask, stroking her mound, so soft and smooth, it's going to taunt me for the rest of my life, even in sleep.

"Yes," she murmurs.

A rough sound crawls out of my mouth. Son of a bitch. On some unconscious level she *was* playing with me, needing this as much as I do. "You're a goddamn cock tease, keeping me in a state of arousal until I broke. Now it's your turn to break, Jenna. Your turn to shatter completely around my tongue and cock." She's visibly vibrating by the time I finish telling her what I plan to do to her, and her nails are clawing at me as I dip my head, slide my finger along her tight slit, and free her clit.

I lap at her, then flatten my tongue for a long slow lick. She's moaning and writhing, a hot mess, lost in lust. I fucking love it. I harden my tongue; whip her clit with accurate precision, until she's pulsating, rocking against me, crying out my name. I tear my tongue away and go lower, to drive into her tight hole as I press my thumb to her clit. I fuck her with the soft blade of my tongue, and apply more pressure to her quivering clit as I ravage her.

"I . . . oh, yes, don't . . . don't stop." She's panting, tossing her head from side to side, and tugging my hair as she squirms.

I continue the dual assault, and she closes her hands over her breasts, so sexy. She makes a noise, hot sexy primal noise as she grinds against me. I fuck her harder, deeper, until she's burning up. My cock throbs, a red-hot rod desperate to feel her sweet cunt wrapped around it. I glance up at her and her mouth opens, but no sound comes as she climaxes. Yeah, that's it, that's the look I love on her.

She comes all over my tongue and fingers, and I want to bath my cock in it, rub it all over the long length of my shaft and let her lick it clean. But I can't get in her just yet, not with her shorts still on. I swirl my fingers in her hot juice, as she clenches, her sex muscles biting down on my probing tongue. I stay with her, until she rides out the orgasm, then I pet her lightly and climb up her body. I kiss her mouth, hard, feverish. Fierce. Demanding. I want her lips swollen, when I pound her into the next decade.

I break from her, and we're both panting, shaking, as I fall to the mattress beside her. I peel off my jeans, and kick off my boots. "Get that tank top off." Through her shirt, I rub my thumb over her nipples. "These need my mouth." She peels her top off, her bra quickly following.

"Climb on top of me, put them in my mouth."

On her hands and knees she crawls toward me. Christ, she looks so damn sexy. I decide then and there that I'm going to fuck her in that position. Yeah, I'm going to edge in behind her, spread her legs wide and push into her, long, hot, deep strokes that will leave us both bruised and sated.

She falls over my naked body, and reality slips away. I'm less than a gentleman in this dream as I grip her ribcage and slide her up until I have her right where I want her. She braces her hands on the mattress over my head, and I suck on one hard nipples. She moans and spread her legs, her hot center pressed against my chest. I smell her arousal, her sweetness as she rubs her pussy all over me.

I lick and suck and bite down on her nipples until their raw and branded. *Mine.* She's moaning, and my body is so tight I'm not going to last long. Hungry with need, I push on her shoulders, and she slides down my body, until she's positioned between my legs.

"Suck me, Jenna. Show me how much you want my cock."

As my body hums with need, she takes my cock in her hand, and devours me with her eyes. I nearly come. Everywhere she touches fills me with warmth and unearths things inside me. Her fingers curl around my girth, and she strokes. I growl, fire licking over my thighs. She bends forward and her breath is so hot against my cock it throbs in her soft palms. I bite back a curse as her pretty pink tongue flicks out. She moans, and licks my crown like it's a goddamn ice cream cone. More precum spills and she greedily laps at it.

"That's it," I bite out and she widens her mouth to accommodate my girth. I push her hair back to watch. Fucking beautiful. "Jesus that's good," I growl. Her hands go to my balls. They tighten. Draw up. Scream for mercy.

I'm a fucking goner.

My cock stabs her mouth and I tug on her hair, needing her to continue almost as much as I need her to stop. "You're fucking killing me," I growl.

That seems to drive her on. She adjusts her body and takes me impossibly deeper, her hands working my shaft and balls. I draw in a breath and try to keep it together. I want to splash down her throat, want all my cum in her, but I'm desperate to get into that tight pussy. Later. Yeah, later I'll come in her mouth. "Stop," I say and curl her hair around my hand three times. "I need to fuck you."

Her eyes are glazed when they meet mine, and my heart thumps, thrilled to know I put that look on her face. She crawls off me, her sweet ass in the air. Lord fucking help me.

"Stay on your hands and knees. I want to fuck you just like that."

She obeys, and I fish a condom from my pocket. I roll it on and rub my cock against her ass. I slide an arm around her, hug her under her breasts and tug until she's upright, but still on her knees. I run my hands over her, slide them down her belly. She moves against me, breathing so hard now, so desperate for my cock, it does something dangerous to me. I slide my hands lower, to touch her wet sex as I kiss her neck, lick the sweetness from her damp skin. She cries out, and arches. My cock presses against the long slit of her ass and I rake my teeth over her skin.

I circle her clit. She quakes around me, and I shove a finger inside her. I stroke deep, and she shatters again. I've barely touched her and she's coming all over me again. Jesus, she's so responsive. Her hand closes over mine, and when she takes it to her mouth and sucks my finger, licking her sweet cum, it's more than I can take.

"Sean," she whispers.

"Yeah."

"I need you to fuck me."

And just like that, I nearly shoot my load. Son of a bitch. Why again, did I insist she tell me when she needs to be fucked? Hearing her saying it, hearing the plea in her voice, is hot as fuck, and arouses the beast in me.

I grip the back of her neck, and bend her over until she's back on her hands and knees. My mind is reeling, intoxicated in her. I growl deep, ready to fuck the hell out of her until we're both a quivering mess. Need. Pure fucking primal need pulls at me.

"Are you desperate for my cock?" Jesus, is that my voice? I sound like I've eaten a handful of the nails in my tool belt.

"Yes," she whimpers.

"Spread for me. I need you wide open."

She parts her knees and wiggles her ass as her body opens to me. I go back on my heels to see her sex, take in the way it glistens invitingly. She has the prettiest pussy, and as I look at it, three words come to mind—mine to own.

I reposition, grip my cock and press it against her sex and she tries to shimmy backward, but I clamp my hand over her slim hip and hold her still. In one swift move I power my hips forward and go balls deep into her lethal softness, stretching her to the hilt as I ram into her soaked opening.

"Fuck," I growl as she sucks me in, her sweet cunt hugging me so nicely. Perfection. Goddamn fucking perfection. I close my eyes against the flood of heat as I pull out, only to slide back in again. Her body shudders around my cock, the vibrations going right through me.

I run my hands along her back, then grip her hips for leverage. I pound into her, and my breath grows shallow as mind-blowing sensations grip my balls. Perspiration breaks out on my body as I continue to spear her with my hard cock, reaching a fevered pitch that takes me to the edge of oblivion in record time.

"Yes," she cries out tension rising in her body curling around me. Delirious with need, pleasure, I give her what she wants. Christ, sex with her the second time is even better yet not nearly enough to sate my cravings.

Told you so.

But how is that even possible?

"Fuck me. Just like that," she adds, rearing back to meet my every hard thrust.

My body shakes, revels in the bliss in her voice. One hand slides up her back, tangles in her hair and I tug until I can hear her screaming my name. Heat floods me, and I reach around her, press my finger to her clit. She grinds against it, the thrust back to meet my every vicious pump.

"I'm . . ." Her voice falls off as she quakes.

Her body shudders around me, her heat scorching my aching cock as she orgasms again. I fuck her furiously, the hot friction whipping around me and escalating the need. Tension snaps. Blood flows thick and heavy. A hot ball of pleasure settles in my groin as I bury the long length of my shaft inside.

Air leaves my lungs in a rush as I fill my rubber with my cum, wishing I was filling her instead. My fingers bite into her hips hard enough to leave a mark. I feel a flash of possessiveness that catches me off guard. Probably because this was the hottest, craziest fucking sex I've ever had, but it was so much more than that.

Somewhere in the distance, near the shore, I hear the waves lapping, teens yelling. It jostles me back to the present and I suck in a breath to get my brain working again. It's crazy how I'd been so lost in her that I hadn't even realized life was going on around us. I pull out of her, fall to the mattress and drag her down with me. I go onto my side, balance on one elbow and brush her hair back, to take in her flushed face. Jesus, I want her again. This second time should have been enough, but I'll be damned if it was.

I poke the mattress. "You ready to let me help you carry this thing inside?" I ask.

She blinks, and confused whiskey-colored eyes go wide as she looks around, like she's trying to orient herself. "Sean, I can't believe we just . . ."

"Had sex outside on the mattress?"

"Yeah, I mean, my neighbors, the beach—"

"Yeah, we probably shouldn't have. Tell you what. Let's me get this inside, and to your bedroom, where we'll have no worries about anyone stumbling in to your front yard and catching us."

Her eyes fill with lust, and she blinks, like she's rethinking this whole thing, but I can't let her do that. She's hot for me, I'm hot for her, so why shouldn't we just keep on having sex—at least until I finish work on her house. Then I'll get my life in order.

"I want to keep fucking you." She goes quiet, lost in thought, an uneasy look moving over her face like she's battling with herself. I'm sure she's running from something but goddammit I don't want her running from me. At least not yet. "Until the job is finished," I add.

Yeah, yeah, I know. My plan to concentrate on the business, set an example for my brothers, and not fuck around with some woman has been severely crippled. But Summer Wheeler—Jenna Garridy—she's no ordinary woman. And therein, of course, lies the problem.

$$\textbf{7}$$

SUMMER

I can't believe I just had sex with Sean, again, and he's talking about more. I should say no. I want to say no but he's like an addiction, and after one taste I can't seem to quit him. Truthfully, I feel less edgy, antsy, scared when he's around. He's rough and tough and wild in the bedroom—or on a mattress in the front yard—but damn, when I'm in his arms I feel safe and untouchable.

"I . . ." His gaze moves over mine, hot, delicious, so tempting. He's waiting for a reaction, a sign that I want more.

"Say yes," he murmurs.

"I . . . have to be at work in an hour," I say.

His grin is wicked, so full of filthy promises, a heated quiver moves through me. Even if I wanted to, there is no way I can fight the chemistry between us.

"Then you'd better get showered." He slides from me, hands me my shorts and tugs on his jeans. I told him I had to work, and it's the truth. But he knows. He knows by the look on my face that this isn't the last time we're going to fall into bed together.

Good God, what am I doing?

I pull on my clothes, except for my bra and panties, but don't get up. "Sean?"

"Yeah."

I take a breath, let it out slowly, and say, "I'm not looking for a relationship." I tug on the frayed edges of my shorts. "I just got out of a bad one."

He stiffens, every muscle in his body so taut, I think something might snap. "Did he hurt you? So help him if he hurt you."

I give a quick shake of my head, shocked at this possessive side of him, even though I shouldn't be. As a kid Sean was always protective, of his brothers, cousins . . . of me. While I'd like to tell him about Jack, or that I had to flush Summer Wheeler's life down the drain for survival. I can't drag him into my troubles. This is my problem, not his, and from the sounds of things around town, he has enough on his plate rounding up his family and getting his father's business back in the black.

"I'm fine," I lie. "I just came here to get my life in order." Not a lie.

He scowls as he stares at me, a good hard glower, like he knows I'm keeping something from him. "How long are you staying?"

"Not sure yet. At least a few months." Until I find the ledger, and figure out what to do with it, I'll be staying. But of course I'm not about to voice that either. He holds his hand out, and I slide my palm into it. I let him pull me to my feet and my body collides with his. He brushes my hair from my face, tender, soft, a barely there caress. My heart stills. Honest to God, somehow that touch feels more intimate than what we just did.

My breasts swell again, my body going hot for him. I put my hand on his shoulder and his muscles ripples, the heat between us volatile. His jaw clenches and he looks like he's fighting some internal battle.

"Jenna," he begins, then goes quiet for a long moment. He shakes his head and says, "You'd better get cleaned up."

I step away from him, but get the sense he wanted to say something else to me. I feel his eyes on my backside, burning in to me and turning me on all over again as I make my way toward the door. I turn, and find him staring, but he doesn't even try to hide it. Moisture beads on his body, as he stands there, hot, mouthwateringly sexy. A shudder overtakes me and I grip the hem of the tank top, a dirty, delicious idea forming as I tug on it. What I'm about to do isn't smart, or rational, but I can't seem to stop myself. His gaze drops to my mouth and desire flares through me.

"Have you heard about the recent water shortage?" I ask.

He arches a brow, his gaze slowly moving back to mine. "A water shortage? Here in Blue Bay?"

"Yes, it's all everyone is talking about."

"Funny how I never heard, then."

"From what I understand, we're supposed to keep water use to a minimum, so I was thinking . . ."

He walks toward me, his grin so dirty and lethal, my knees nearly give. How is it possible that we just had sex and I want him again, so soon? Normally I can go weeks, months even without ever being touched, but with him, if I don't feel his hand all over me in the next few minutes I might go up in flames.

"Go on," he says.

"Well, since we're both hot and sweaty and we're both in need of a shower, I thought we could help the environment, by showering together."

He takes one last step, and I yelp in surprise when he scoops me up, and carries me into the house.

"I do like how you're concerned about the environment," he says, "I'm quite environmentally conscious myself."

He sets me onto the sink, reaches into the small shower stall, and turns on the water. He unbuttons his jeans and kicks them, as well as his boots, off again. My mouth waters as he stands before me, completely naked, not a hint of modesty about him. I look him over, and he comes closer, bracing his hands on the counter top on either side of my thighs. His mouth is close, his warm breath washing over my face. I take in his hard body—one clearly made for sin—and trace the scorpion tattoo.

I don't think I'll ever tire of seeing him naked. "Does this have meaning?"

"Yeah."

I wait for him to answer, when he doesn't, I touch his scars, run my finger over their purple surfaces. "How did you get all these?"

"Motocross racing."

As the water heats up, steam fills the room. I blink at him, then touch the deep mark near his jugular. "This one looks bad."

"I lived."

"Yeah, but I think you have a death wish," I say quietly.

"Some would say I do."

"Why . . . why did you come back to Blue Bay?"

He stiffens, and runs his hands through his hair as he turn from me. I take in his tension, intensity. "Had some family things to take care of."

I touch his chin, bringing his gaze back to me. "Like running your dad's business?"

"What do you know about that?"

"Small town. I work at the local bar. You hear things."

"Why did you come back?"

"As you know, I'd been here a few times with Summer."

This time I look away. It's hard to keep secrets from Sean. "I thought it would be good place to hang out as I got my life in order."

"Because of the ex."

"Yeah."

"Is that it, or is there anything else you want to tell me?"

"That's it," I say.

He puts his hand on my face, and I angle my chin to see him. His eyes are darker, a deeper shade of green as they move over my face, a careful assessment. I don't really think for one minute I'm fooling him. He knows who I am, but he's not saying anything. Not only am I grateful that he's keeping my secret, it proves he's trustworthy, and I need someone like that in my life right now.

His warm breath washes over me, and my insides flutter, all thoughts of my troubles dissipating beneath his hands. He grips the hem of my top, and peels it over my head. A tortured look crosses his face as he gazes at my breasts. He bends, presses a soft kiss to each one, then picks me up like I weigh nothing, and sets me back on the floor. He drops to his knees, and slides my shorts to my ankles. I lift my feet, one at a time and he discards the shorts.

He stands back up and looks me over. "You're so beautiful." His eyes go to mine and turn serious. "I don't want to stop fucking you." I swallow. "There are so many things I want to do to you, so many ways I want to take you." My pulse speeds up and my legs nearly go out from underneath me.

"Sean—"

He steps into me. "For the rest of the summer, you're mine."

"You said until the end of the job."

"Changed my mind."

Tension arcs between us, thick as the steam curling

around the room "Are you asking for a summer fling?" I question, my voice too shaky, husky.

"Yes." His body is tense, tormented as he dips his head, and brushes his thumb over my bottom lip. "Nothing more."

The idea of having him in my bed for the next month, feeling his big, strong arms around me, giving me a sense of comfort as he fucks me is deliciously tempting.

"Say yes."

I should say no. I want to say no. This is Sean Owens, dangerous to my heart in so many ways, and I'm lying to him about my identity for God's sake. Not only that, I can't—won't—drag him into my world.

But honest to God, how often does an offer like this come around. I'd be crazy to so no, right.

"Just casual sex?"

"Just casual. Unless you want formal. But I really don't like fucking in a tuxedo."

A sexy dimple flashes as he grins, and I laugh as I turn to step into the stall. He climbs in behind me, and I shift to make room for his large body. He crowds me, hovers close as the warm, needle like spray falls over us.

I grab the soap, about to lather my body when he takes it from me. Bubbles form in his palms and he sets the bar down and runs his big, callused hands over my flesh.

"One more thing," he says as he turns me. His hands touch my shoulders, feather down my back, and he cups my cheeks.

"What?" I ask.

"You let me do things for you."

"You are doing things for me. You're fixing my house."

"That's not what I'm talking about."

"No?"

"No."

"Sean, I'm not your responsibility."

"Maybe not, but it's like this, when you need a damn mattress picked up, or anything else, you ask."

"Like how you want me to ask when I want you to fuck me?"

He goes still behind me and I can't help but grin. It secretly thrills me to know I can reduce this big, monster of a guy speechless.

He clears his throat. "Yeah, like that." I wiggle my ass and he growls in my ear. "If you keep that up, I'm going to fuck this sweet ass of yours."

Now it's my turn to go still. "I've never—"

"I know," he says, and rakes his teeth over my shoulder. "How much time do we have before you have to work?"

His hard cock presses against my back. "Half hour."

"I'll be fast," he says.

Dizzy with need, I turn to him, run my hands over his body. "Fast works," I say, much too anxious to feel him inside me again. I touch his cock and quiver as he swells even more. It's big and hard, and—designed solely for my pleasure. He reaches between my legs and thrusts two fingers deep inside me. My knees go weak and he turns my body, and wraps a strong, supportive arm around me. He plunges deep, and presses his palm to my needy clit. I clutch at his arms and rock my hips.

"God, Sean."

"I need to be in here," he murmurs, as he bends to rake his teeth over my shoulder. "Tell me you need that, too."

"I need that too," I say my voice coming out on a breathless whisper. He pulls his fingers from me, and spins me back to face him. He grips my hips and lifts me and I wrap my legs around him and he backs me up until I'm pressed against the shower, the hot water on his back. His eyes are dark, hard, dangerously ravenous as he shifts me, the long length of his cock pressing against my sex. He's hard as hard as granite, like we hadn't just had sex outdoors. I wiggle, trying to get him inside, but then still completely, when little alarm bells jangle in my brain.

"Sean, wait."

He presses his forehead against mine. "Jesus fuck, please tell me you're not having second thoughts."

"No. It's just . . . condom . . . you're not wearing a condom."

"Shit, you're right."

He loosens his hold on me but I squeeze my legs around him to prevent him from leaving. "Wait. I'm on the pill, and I'm clean."

What am I doing?

He meets my gaze, looks me over. "I'm clean, too. I've never had unprotected sex before. You can trust me."

Do I trust Sean? Yes, I do. I always have. But I won't burden him with my problems.

I press my mouth to his, and as he kisses me back, he powers into me. I gasp.

"You feel so fucking good," he murmurs, as he rocks his hips. My breasts rub against his chest with each hard thrust, and my clit slams against his pelvis. I can't move, I can't breathe, all I can do is hang on with my hands and legs as he fucks me fast.

"I want my cum inside you," he growls, his mouth on my neck, tasting, licking, nipping. "I've never needed my cum in anyone, but I need it in you."

My breath is coming faster now, and no way am I going to analyze this situation, why he needs his cum in me or why I'm having sex with Sean, no condom, no barriers. Skin on skin. It's a mistake. I know it is, but when I leave Blue Bay, I'll have plenty of time to examine my behavior, the way this man makes me feel so many foreign things. Right now, I just want to enjoy the sensations he's rousing in me.

He slams me against the shower stall, and I scratch at his back as he fucks me hard, harder than ever before, like he's running from his demons on the open highway, full throttle on his motorcycle.

"Yes," I cry out, and his mouth closes over mine to capture the sound. Our tongues tangle, play, thrash as we exchange greedy kisses that will leave us bruised. He works me up and down on his cock and I heave in a breath, my body near the breaking point. The rough scruff on his face chafes my neck and I love the sensations. Lightning flashes through me, crashes over me, and I shudder in surrender.

"Sean," I cry out as I explode. I shake around his cock, shatter completely. He holds me as I ride it out the waves, then his fingers fist in my wet hair.

"Don't move," he growls and I still as his cock fills with blood and swells even more inside me. He rocks into me once, twice, then throws his head back.

"Ooh," I cry out as hot seed fills me, warming my body from the inside out. I have never felt pleasure quite like it. I sigh, and rest my head on his shoulder, and he peppers my neck with hot, openmouthed kisses.

"Every time, just like that," he murmurs against my flesh.

I laugh, giddy with endorphins. "If you're promising that, I'll never get to work."

His rumble of laughter falls over my flesh, and he inches back. "Right. Work."

I slide from his body, and instantly miss his warmth. Not wanting to think too much about that, I slip back under the spray, but the water has chilled. I yelp, rinse quickly, and climb out. Sean follows me, and grabs a big fluffy towel off the hook. He wraps me in it, and gives me a slap on the ass to set me into motion.

"You'd better hurry or you're going to be late."

I rush from the room, but my feet come to a resounding

halt when I hear my cell phone ringing from the depths of my purse in the other room. I stand there, my heart hammering against my chest. In my haste to get away from Jack, I never took the time to cancel my phone or change the number. Then, after having a landline installed here at the cottage, I never gave it another thought, since I had no intentions of using it and risk getting tracked. If it's Jack calling does he really think I'm stupid enough to answer.

"Jenna," Sean says, his hand brushing my arm, his solid chest against my back, providing comfort, support.

"Yeah?" I ask without turning. No way do I want Sean to see my face. He's too good at reading me.

"Are you going to get that?"

"No."

He spins me around and our gazes tangle. I meet with eyes that are dark, dangerous . . . murderous. Body rigid, agitated, the muscles along his jaw clench, the way they always do when he's troubled. "Are you sure there isn't something you want to tell me?"

I open my mouth, wanting to tell this big, strong protective man my troubles, but they're *my* troubles not his, and even though he makes me feel safe, I can't put all this on him.

Instead of blurting out the truth I say, "I'm sure." My phone stops ringing and I exhale a breath I wasn't even aware I was holding. Towel wrapped around me, I walk to the kitchen, to find my phone. I glance at the number, but it looks like it's some telemarketer. I make light of the situation and say, "No one knows the number so I figured it had to be telemarketer. That's why I didn't answer."

Sean knots his towel around his waist and takes the phone from me. Before I can stop him, he slides his finger over the screen to open it, then punches in his contact information. Then he pulls up mine. "Now I know the number and you have mine." He hands it back. "Now, next time it rings, you might not be so spooked."

"Wait," I say. "Use my landline." I grab a piece of paper, jot down the number and hand it to him.

"Is there some reason you don't want me using this phone?"

"Data roaming," I say. Dammit, I should have just tossed the phone. "I forgot to look into an add-on plan for here in Blue Bay."

He gives me a look that suggests I might be bending the truth. I am. But no way can I let him know the real reason why he can't call me.

8

SEAN

After two rounds of sex with Summer earlier today—yeah, in my head she's Summer but I'll call her Jenna if that's the way she still wants to play it—I spend the rest of the afternoon at the town council trying to get building permits to do work on the Cassidy place. I hit a wall at every turn, held back by so much red tape I was damn near ready to strangle someone with it. I'm in a pretty pissed-off mood as I sit at table across from my brother, one eye on him, the other on Summer as I suck back a cold beer. I twirl the bottle, take a long pull, then slam it down onto the wooden table much harder than necessary.

"What the fuck is the matter with you anyway?" Tyler asks, flicking a beer cap over and under his fingers. He's as restless and edgy as I am tonight, no doubt itching for a fight.

"You know what's the matter with me," I say.

"We'll get the permits. I'm sure of it."

I'm not, and if we don't get them soon, Tyler won't be able to build the addition to the Cassidy mansion. I've sunk ever cent I earned into the business, and I'll be damned if I let it fail because Walker has them stalling at city hall. I have no proof it's him, of course, but after he learned I wasn't just here to bury dad, but also to get his business up and running again with all the Owens boys returning home, I knew he'd try to find a way to run us out of town. When I saw him coming from city hall, a shit-eating grin on his face, my gut told me he was the one trying to stall things until I ran the business into the ground, and we all rode back to where we came from. He might have a lot of pull, but money goes a long way, too. What I really need is a crap load of bills to go down there and grease some palms.

From the corner of my eye, I watch Summer. Tray in hand, tight jeans hugging her ass to perfection, she's serving two dickless assholes a drink, and I don't fucking like the way they're looking at her. Tyler turns to see what's really getting under my skin.

His grin is wide when he turns back to me. "You got something going with Jenna?"

I glare at him. No way would he remember her. He was too young back in the day and she's changed drastically. "So what if I do?"

He holds his hands up, arms out. "Hey, just asking." He nods toward the assholes and cracks his knuckles, ready and prepared to pounce at my word. "Want me to help you put their eyes back in their head?"

"Yeah, I fucking want you to." I eye my little brother. How long will he last here in Blue Bay? No action, no fighting, just good old hard work with a hammer instead of his fists? We've all carved out our own paths in life, none of which involved Blue Bay. I called them all back for the funeral, and to help with the business, but I can't expect them to give up their lives because I need to be the man Dad needs me to be. If only I had done it sooner, made him proud, but no I was too fucking busy out satisfying my own urges and avoiding the disappointed look on his scowling face. And now that I am back, I should be paying more attention to living up to my responsibilities, and less time thinking about sweet Summer Wheeler.

Ty pushes from the table and is about to get up when I give a slow shake of my head. "Not in here," I say. Summer has only been working here for a week and I don't want to get her in any kind of shit with Beck. He's a good guy, we go way back, and I respect his one rule: No fighting in Winchesters.

Outside, however.

The heavy oak door opens with a bang and my mood lightens when I see Jamie saunter in like he's on fucking vacation. He glances around, and the corner of his mouth turns up when he spots us in the far corner, our backs to the wall so we can take in everything.

I lift my beer in salute, and he walks over. Both Ty and I jump up to hug our brother.

I let Ty go first, then grip Jamie's T-shirt and pull him in. "About fucking time you got here." We exchange a hard hug.

"Unlike you two assholes, I had a life and shit to take care of before I could come home."

I look him over, take in his body art. Who would have thought that my little brother would grow up to be an amazing tattoo artist? "I'm glad you're here," I say. With only a year separating us in age, Jamie and I were tight growing up. We did everything together, and I miss him like fuck. But like me, he left here years ago, tired of taking shit from the old man, tired of disappointing him. Yeah, sure, Dad was a pillar of society, like by everyone, but he rode his sons hard. Everyone knew it. What I realize now, but didn't know back then, was that he was just trying to fill the role of both father and mother and make strong men of us—except none of us responded well to his methods. I pull Jamie back in.

"It's good to be home," he says, his voice slightly broken, fractured as he fists my shirt. I work to keep my shit together as I pull back to see him again. He might be a mean mother-fucker, in with the gangs down in New Orleans, but when it comes to family, there isn't anything he wouldn't do to protect them.

We stare, but no words need to be said. He has a shit storm going on inside him every bit as much as the rest of us.

His throat works as he swallows, and he looks at his boots. "I should have come sooner."

"Yeah," I say. We all should have. "Well you're here now and that's all that matters."

He looks from me to Ty, then back to me. "Who's back?"

"Just us three."

"Have you heard from Jared and Jacob?"

I nod, and push back on two legs as I think about the call I made to our twin brothers. They took the news as hard as the rest of us. "They're on their way."

"What about Ryan, Carter, and Jace?"

At the mention of our cousins, who we really consider our brothers, I say, "I called everyone."

He grabs a chair, spins it around, and drops into it. Arms braced on the back, he signals Summer. When she reaches our table, he narrows his eyes and looks her over. "Do I know you?"

"Real fucking original," Ty says, and shoves Jamie.

"Fuck off," Jamie shoots back and shoves Ty in return. He doesn't budge. Instead he laughs and folds his arms across his barrel chest. "Want to take this outside?" he asks.

"Little fucker," Jamie says, and jumps up to grab Ty in a headlock. He rubs his knuckles over Ty's head, in familiar Jamie fashion. Except that might have worked when they were eleven and eight, now not so much. "Need me to show you who's the *big* brother here?" he taunts.

Here we go.

Ty jumps up, spins and turns the table on Jamie. Chairs fly

as he grabs Jamie in a rear naked hold, jumps on his back to lock on, and drags him to the floor. Someone squeals, their drink flying as the two wrestle around on the ground.

Summer backs up, her eyes wide, and I reach for her hand. Her gaze shoots to mine as I stand and put her behind me. "It's okay," I say. "This goes way back to when they were kids. Ty owes him a beat-down for the all noogies Jamie gave him."

"Noogies?"

"I take it you don't have brothers," I ask, even though I already know the answer.

"No, only child."

I keep her behind me and she goes up on her toes to see over my shoulder as the guys roughen each other up. After Summer's mom died, and she left here with her father, I lost track of her. I don't even know if her father is still alive. Jesus, what would he do if he found out Sean Owens was fucking his little girl? He was always protective of her, and rarely let her out of his sight when he was here in Blue Bay and not out on a naval ship, patrolling our waters.

He was gone that time I dragged her from the water and gave her mouth-to-mouth. Her mom was on the beach, chatting with her friends, when Summer got a cramp and took in water. When her old man arrived he paid me a visit, told me to stay the fuck away from his daughter. Man, I'd just saved his little girl and that was his response. Then again, I had a reputation a mile long, and was a poster boy for authority issues, so in a way I can't blame the man. I guess fathers protect their daughters, and I can't hold that against him. What he'd failed to realize is that I'd never let anything happen to his daughter—back in the day, or now. Then again, maybe I didn't want him to see me as anything different, maybe I let him see the worse it me because I feared I couldn't live up to his expectation either.

Regardless, no matter what I was doing, swimming, hanging with my brothers, or tearing up the streets, I'd always kept an eye on her. Most times Jamie was with me. I think he knew all about my secret crush. Now that I know she's on the run, and there are things she's not telling me, I plan to keep her in my line of sight until I feel her safety is no longer an issue.

The two guys who'd been eye fucking Summer are looking at my brothers with fear in their eyes. Yeah, they should be scared. I scoff. Those are the kinds of guys Summer's dad would want her with. Old Blue Bay money. But look at them. One ounce of trouble and they're pissing in their pants.

I steal a glance around, take in the group of girls sipping their martinis and getting off on this shit. No doubt my brothers will have one of them warming their beds tonight. Ty gets Jamie on the ground, his arm behind his back as he slams his shoulder into the floor.

"Tap out, bro, or I'll break it."

"Son of a bitch," Jamie says, and twists, trying to get out of the hold, but no way can he budge the two hundred pounds and then some of solid muscle holding him down. He's such a stubborn bastard, however, that no way is he going to tap out. Ty will choke hold him until he passes out first. Only problem is a few patrons are getting worked up—they don't know my brothers are play-fighting. One look at them and you'd think they were trying to kill each other. But since I don't want any trouble with the law, I need to break this shit up.

I move Summer back out of the way, so she doesn't get hit with a flailing arm or leg. She reaches for me, curls her fingers in my shirt and the way she looks to me for protection has my insides coiling. I like being her protector. "Don't worry, I won't let anything happen to you." She looks at me with those big eyes like she wants to believe me, *needs* to believe me, then nods her head and lets her hands fall to her sides.

"I'm a big girl. I can take care of myself."

"I know but while I'm around, that's going to be my job," I say. I don't wait for a response, won't tolerate hearing no on her lips. Instead I kick Ty in the ribs, not hard enough to hurt, but with enough power behind it to get his attention. "Finish it."

Ty grins. "Tap out big brother."

"Fuck you," Jamie says.

I reach for Ty, but when I do, a bolt of pain shoots from my shoulder down to my back. "Christ," I winch, and Summer steps back into me. "Are you okay?"

"Yeah, just overdid it today on the roof."

She sets her tray on the table and puts those soft hands on me. "Let me see." She feels around a bit, and pulls on my arm, moving it back and forth, then she steps behind me and runs her hands along my spine.

"You need an adjustment. Tomorrow before you start on the roof, I'll try to help you work out the kink."

At the mention of "kink," my dick goes hard, and I'm guessing by the blush moving into her cheeks, she knows she picked the wrong choice of words.

"Kink?" I tease. "Don't toy with me, Jenna, or there will be consequences."

Heat colors her face, and I step into her, crowd her, let her know I'm ready to fuck again, right here right now.

"I . . . I mean . . ."

I angle my head, stare at her lush lip, all humor gone from my voice when I ask, "What do you know about adjustments?"

"I . . . uh . . ." She stalls, like she's trying to backtrack, but I won't have any of that. "Well, my friend is a chiropractor, and she taught me a few tricks, and I think I could . . ."

I glare at her and her voice falls off. How many more lies is she going to spill? Fuck, why is it that she thinks she can't trust me with her secrets? Especially when she trusts me with her body.

Oh, probably because of my reputation, my authority issues, and I did tell her one-night stands were my specialty—and they were, until she came back into my life. But she's running from her ex—by rights I should hunt the prick down and beat the fuck out of him for putting her on the defense like this—and I'm not the kind of guy she'd ever want anything more with. She has white picket fence, minivan, and 2.4 kids in her future. No way will you catch me behind the wheel of a minivan, and when it comes to a kid, that's where I tap out. What do I know about parenting? I'd end up fucking them up. All I ever had was a hard-ass, brutal son of a bitch teaching me how to be a man.

Officer Walker steps into the bar, and when he sees my brother's on the floor, he puts his hands over his gun. Shit. My foul mood returns and I grab Ty and haul him off Jamie. Walker saunters over to us.

"Problem here?" he asks.

"Nope, just saying hello to Jamie," Ty says, and straightens to his full height, an intimidating bastard, but Walker doesn't intimidate easily. Why would he when he's the law with a gun at his side.

"I told Sean and I'm telling you. I don't want no trouble."

Summer shifts behind me and grabs her tray off the table. She scurries to the bar, and Stacey meets her. Stacey nods my way, then says something to Summer. I can't hear the exchange from my distance, but I'm sure the other waitress is filling her in on the Owens boys—and probably warning her to stay away. Years ago, Stacey had a thing with one of the twins and has been pissed off ever since.

"We're not looking for trouble," Jamie says through

gritted teeth and I can tell it's taking all his restraint not to get up in Walker's face.

Walker turns to me, that same shit-eating grin on his face. "How's business?"

I fold my arms across my chest. "Booming."

He scoffs. "That so?" he asks.

"That's so."

He turns, and strolls up to the bar. He speaks to the bartender Adam, then walks out of the place, taking a moment to cast us another warning look. What-the-fuck-ever. The man is really starting to piss me off.

"I need a fucking beer," Jamie says. He gestures to Summer again and when she arrives he narrows his eyes and glares at Ty in warning before slowly turning to her. He gives her another once-over, his gaze roaming over those freckles that make her look so adorable. "So I do know you, right?" he asks.

Ty smirks and a snicker sounds in his throat. I join Jamie in glaring at him. He raises his hands in surrender and mouths the words, "Fine."

"No, I'm Jenna Garridy. I'm a friend of Summer Wheeler's. You're probably just confusing us," Summer says.

A pause, his thumb tapping a beat on the wood table. Even though he still doesn't look convinced he shrugs and says, "Yeah, that must be it."

Summer's fingers fumble with the notepad in her hand. "What can I get you?"

He circles his finger. "A round for us all."

She nods and dashes to the bar. I could tell Jamie she really is Summer Wheeler, but I don't. She's keeping her identity a secret for a reason, one I'm certain has everything to do with her ex. So help the bastard if he shows up here in Blue Bay. He won't just have one Owens brother to contend with, he'll have a brotherhood, an army. Not that there will be anything left for my brothers once I'm through with him. But for now, I'll keep her identity a secret and I'll keep her in my crosshairs to make sure she's safe.

"Been by to see Gram?" Ty asks Jamie. As the two fall into conversation, I push away from the table. I pass by the booth where the two dickless assholes are sitting. How dare they have the nerve to eye fuck my girl. *My girl?* Well for the remainder of the season she is anyway. While I'd like to punch those douchebags in the face, I don't want to cause trouble for Summer, but that doesn't mean I'm not going to stake my fucking claim on her.

She has her back to me at the bar. I slide in behind her, put my hands on either side of the bar top and press my mouth to her ear. "I can't wait to be inside you again," I say, and her body shudders as I cage her with mine.

"Sean," she whispers, and her hands shake as she puts a drink on her tray.

I inch back so she can turn. Her eyes darken with desire when they see me, and I brush her bottom lip with my thumb. "Actually, this is where I want my cock next time."

She darts a quick glance around, but no one can hear me, and because my body is blocking hers, no one can see the way she's rubbing up against me like a kitten. Next time I get her into bed, she'd better fucking purr for me.

"I . . . I need to work," she says.

"Okay, but if those little fuckers give you any trouble, you better let me know, and my brothers and I will take this shit outside."

"Those two. Don't worry. I've dealt with the likes of their kind before. I used to waitress in college."

"College?"

Her eyes go wide. Clearly, she just told me something she hadn't meant to. Jesus, she has so many secrets. I should ask, I want to ask, but she doesn't want to fucking tell me. Guess she doesn't trust me enough. That bugs the shit out of me, but since I only asked for a casual affair, she doesn't owe me anything more than that. That doesn't mean I'm not going to watch over her though.

"I . . . yeah . . . long time ago."

"Yeah, well. I don't like the way they're looking at you. If they make you uncomfortable at all. Let me know."

"Sean," she says. Fuck man, I love hearing my name on her lips.

"Yeah?"

"I think you just made it pretty clear to them not to mess with me."

I grin. "Yeah, I guess I did."

Her pouty lips turn up and my dick hardens even more. "I need to deliver these drinks."

I dip my head and lightly brush my mouth over hers. She sucks in a feathery breath, and I step to the side to clear her path. I follow her back to the table, and take my seat. And we start to get caught up in each other's lives as we shoot back our beer.

An hour later, Jamie stretches and says, "I need to go see Gram before she goes to bed."

"Yeah, come on."

I stand but when I do the girls drinking the margaritas saunter up to us, giggling, and twirling their hair around their fingers. I shake my head. Every girl, in every town. All the fucking same. My gaze slides to Summer who is watching the girls touch us.

She's not the same.

"You guys going somewhere?" the pretty blonde asks, her hand on Jamie's arm.

Jamie grins. "Yeah, but we'll be back."

She pouts. "I thought you might want to play a game of pool."

"We'll play," Ty says. "Just not tonight."

I look them over. Any other night I might have taken them up on their offer. Now, the only woman I want in my bed is Summer. I cast her a glance again and when my eyes meet hers she jerks away, and goes back to filling her tray with drinks. I follow my brothers out the door, and the girls are close behind. They stand there grinning, and blatantly staring as I jump into the truck and Ty climbs into the passenger seat. He jacks the tunes and taps his fingers on the dashboard as I drive home, Jamie following on his Harley.

Gram is in the kitchen on her laptop, surfing Facebook when we enter. Gotta love a seventy-year-old who keeps up with technology. She jumps up when she sees we have Jamie with us.

"Jamie, my sweet boy," she says, and he picks her up for a hug. Her long white nightgown flares around her ankles. "Come in, come in. Are you hungry?"

He rubs his gut. "Starved."

"Hey what about me?" Ty says. "I'm hungry, too."

Her green eyes crinkle and she reaches up to pinch Ty's cheeks.

"You're always hungry." She turns to me, but I'm focused on the computer. Would Summer have a Facebook account? If so, I might be able to track her asshole ex through it, and pay him a visit.

"You hungry, Sean?" she asks again.

"No I'm good, Gram."

She folds her arms in familiar Gram fashion. "Something on your mind?"

"Yeah, Jenna Garridy. The new waitress at Winchesters."

I spin and glare at my baby brother, but he's grinning like the damn village idiot, and unlike Jamie he has no idea Jenna is Summer and is on the run.

"Oh, a girl." Gram winks at me. "I'll have to make a visit to Winchesters."

"No, Gram. She's just a friend."

Ty mouths the words, "One you're fucking," and I make a mental note to smother him when he's sleeping tonight. Gram hurries to the fridge, and I walk to the cupboard, grab some pain meds and toss them back. Damn shoulder is aching like a bitch tonight. I should probably ask one of the guys to help with the roof, but then I wouldn't have Summer all to myself, mine to fuck anytime we like.

I leave Gram and the guys in the kitchen, and head to the bathroom for a hot shower. The water feels good against my aching muscles, and I stay under until it turns cold. I towel off and walk to my room. I fall onto my bed and stare at the ceiling. Hours later sleep still doesn't come, so I tug on my jeans and head to Jamie's room. I knock.

"Yeah."

Looks like I'm not the only one who can't sleep. I open the door and shut it behind me. Light from the crack in his curtain slants across the wall, and Jamie shuffles to make room for me. I flop out on the bed bedside him, and jab my hands under my head. We lie like that for a long time, neither talking, but both taking comfort in each other's presence. I missed him so fucking much.

"You good?" I finally ask.

"Yeah, you?"

"Yeah."

He rolls to his side, goes up on one elbow, his eyes dark, dangerous—murderous. "Is Summer in some kind of trouble?"

I scoff and shake my head. I should have known he'd bring it up sooner or later, and I'm glad he waited until we're alone. "Yeah."

"How bad?"

I mimic his position. "Don't know. She's not talking. But I suspect it has everything to do with her ex."

"Who is he?"

"Don't know that either."

His eyes narrow, zero in on me. "I'm here if you need me."

"Thanks, bro."

I fall back onto the mattress, dead tired after a long day.

"I'll fix the front porch and swing," Jamie says, his voice low as he drifts off to sleep.

"Okay." A pause and then, "Jamie, are you still good with security systems?" He used to work for Eagle Security in New Orleans before opening his own tattoo shop.

"The best."

I laugh. No modesty there. "Tomorrow, can you install one in the old Wheeler home?"

"You got it."

I shut my eyes, visions of Summer in my mind's eye as fatigue pulls at me, my brother's comforting presence lulling me to sleep. But then my phone rings, and the nerves along my back tingle in warning. Something's wrong. I feel it in every fiber of my being. I jackknife up, and pull my cell from my back pocket, and slide my finger across the screen.

"Sean," Summer says, her voice hushed, frightened.

I climb from the bed. "Are you hurt?" I ask.

"There's a noise, outside the window."

"I'm on my way." I turn to Jamie. "I gotta go."

"You need me?"

"I'll let you know."

9

SUMMER

I hug myself as I rush through the cottage to shut the lights out and pull the curtains closed as I wait for Sean to arrive. I wasn't going to call him. I swore I wouldn't involve him, but the loud bang outside my kitchen window sounded like a gunshot. Back in California, such a sound would give me pause, then I'd go on with my daily routine. Here in Blue Bay, gunshots are unheard of and my ex is out there searching for me.

I hear a bike idle down in the driveway, then a pounding on the door and I nearly jump out of my robe. I pad quietly across the room and do the mental math. He couldn't have gotten here this quick. It can't be him. I begin to back away, look for some sort of weapon. My heart and head pound in tandem and it's getting more difficult to draw in air.

"Open up. It's me."

My God, he had to have been going at a breakneck speed to get here so fast. I suck in a breath and hurry to the door. I unlock it and open it to see Sean standing on the other side, tall, powerful an indestructible force to be reckoned. I exhale a quick breath.

He reaches for me, pulls me tight against his body. My legs wobble and I feel light-headed as I come down from the adrenaline rush.

He hugs me and brushes my hair back. "You okay?"

"Yes," I say, clinging to him as if my life depended on it. "I heard a noise. It scared me. I'm sorry for calling so late. I just . . . didn't know who else to call and I didn't mean to interrupt. I saw you with those girls and I was going to call the police, but you don't seem to trust them so . . ."

"Jenna, relax."

I bite my bottom lip. "I should have called the police." Maybe on some deeper level I didn't because I wanted Sean here, with me. The only person I can trust.

"No, you shouldn't have."

"I shouldn't be bothering you."

"You're not bothering me. Calling me was the smart thing to do. Who knows how long it would have taken the police to get here?"

"You got here so fast." I take deep breaths and try to regulate my pulse. "At first I didn't even think it was you."

He holds my shoulders and inches back to see my face. He goes deadly still, his eyes hard, lethal as they glare at me. "Who did you think it was?"

"I . . . uh . . . don't know," I say.

Every muscle in his body tightens at my lie and I redirect before he can call me on it. "I have a feeling if Walker catches you speeding he's going to take you in."

He looks at me, closely, carefully, "Probably, but you needed me, and I did what I had to do to be here for you."

A new tenderness moves over him and I try to ignore it, try to ignore the mushy feelings it arouses in me, but the task is impossible. This is Sean Owens, underneath it all he's a good man, a man who could have any girl he wanted—might have even been with one when I called—and despite all the lies, he dropped everything—for me. Other than my father, no man had ever put me first and I have to say it makes me feel pretty darn peculiar inside.

"And for the record, I was home. In bed. Alone."

"Okay." That shouldn't make me as happy as it does.

"Well, I wasn't exactly alone."

"It's fine." Oh, God, I do not need the details. "You don't owe me an explanation. We don't have—"

"I told you. Me and you. No one else for as long as you're here. I'm a man of my word. I crashed beside my brother, Jamie."

A wave of relief washes over me and I nod.

Strong, solid, never wavering, he eases me inside the house, and shuts the door behind him. Big hands that make me feel so safe go around my body and tug me close. I know I'm getting in too deep with him, but right now I don't care. We stand in the dark, and he holds me for a long time. I sag into him, take comfort in his strength. I breathe with him, my head against his chest, moving slightly against his strong heartbeat.

"Where did you hear the noise?" he asks quietly, breaking the silence.

I lift a shaky finger and point. "Outside the kitchen window."

"I'm going to do a sweep of the inside first, okay?" He puts his hands on my hips and places me against the wall. "Stay here."

Panic bursts inside my stomach. "No," I say quickly. "I want to come with you."

A pause and then, "Okay, stay behind me."

I hold the back of his shirt, as he walks through the cottage like a predator, flicking on lights and checking every dark corner. He makes his way down the hall, opens my childhood bedroom door and goes still.

"Everything okay?" I ask, my nose pressed into his back, breathing in his clean soapy smell.

"Yeah, just . . . everything in here reminds me of Summer." His body tightens. "It's been a long time. It wasn't quite the same around here after she left."

I swallow against the lump punching into my throat, because I miss Summer, too. Pretending to be Jenna is getting harder and harder, especially with Sean, but my father's instructions were to trust no one. I'm hardly following that advice with Sean, though. Back in the day he never liked Sean, and if he knew I was with him now, calling him when I was scared, he'd turn over in his grave.

"Room's clear." He turns, and puts his hand on the knob to my parents' room and a sound catches in my throat. He reaches behind him, gives my hip a squeeze. "You okay?"

"Yes," I lie. The door yawns open like a sealed casket. After searching it earlier, I pinch my eyes shut against the memories, not wanting to look again. Breath held, I recite the alphabet, anything to keep the pain at bay. But I can't. I shake, almost violently.

"Clear in here, too." Sean turns, and I open my eyes to find him watching me. Head dipped, he pulls me to him and presses a kiss to my forehead. His breath is warm on my face, and his hair falls forward to tickle my cheeks. "It's okay. I'm here. Nothing bad is going to happen to you. Ever again."

For a minute I wonder if he's talking about the noise I heard, or does he know what opening that door has done to me, how it's dredged up so many painful past memories? He holds me for a long time, then puts me behind him again.

"One more room," he whispers. The door to the room I'm sleeping in is open and he steps inside. "Come here." He turns, puts his arm around me and leads me to the bed. "The house is clear. I want you to stay here while I check outside."

I nod, grip one of the stuffed toys and hold it to my chest.

He stands there for a long time, just staring at me. "What?" I finally ask.

"Nothing."

He turns to leave and I say, "Be careful."

"I will."

His boots echo on the wood floors, and the front door creaks open and closes with a soft thud. The house goes silent, eerily silent and I hug the toy harder as I wait. A few minutes later a noise finally penetrates the quiet.

"Sean?"

"Yeah, it's me." The heavy front door closes and the lock clicks in place

A fluttery breath escapes my throat. "Okay, good."

He fills the bedroom doorway, the calm in my storm, yet a different kind of storm going on inside him. I feel it in his every breath, his every movement. He, too, is on the run, but my gut tells me his demons live inside him, and no way in hell can he outrun them.

"A raccoon tipped over your garbage cans."

Thank God.

Still, it's a good reminder to never let my guard down, never to think I'm safe. I'm about to stand, thank him, and walk with him back to the front door, but he's tugging his shirt over his head, and kicking off his pants and boots.

"What . . . are you doing?"

"I'm staying," he whispers, rough and low, then pulls his phone from his pocket to send a text.

I stare at the phone. "It's okay, you don't—"

He fires off the text and sets his phone on the nightstand. "Just letting my brother know everything is okay and I'm staying, now get in that bed, or I'll toss you in it."

The last thing I expected was for him to stay the night. Then again, maybe I did but I can't put him out like that. "But—"

His sharp glare stops me, and when he takes a threatening step, I remove my robe, but have only my nightie on underneath, no panties. From the look on his face, I have no time to worry about that. I climb between the sheet and scurry to the other side of the bed. He slides in behind me. "Come here." I shuffle backward, and press against the warm strength of his body. He puts his arms around me and drags me closer. Tension leaves my body and my shoulders relax. At no point in my adult life have I ever felt this protected—and in so many ways that a danger to me.

"Sleep," he whispers against the shell of my ear and I close my eyes. His warmth and comfort pull me under, and the next thing I know, the morning sun is seeping into my room. I blink, and rub my eyes, unable to orient myself. But then I realize I'm at the cottage and Sean slept in my bed with me last night. My heart warms, little flutters erupting in my stomach as I think about the way he'd come to my rescue, spooned me, covering me with his big warm body and comforting touch while I drifted off to sleep.

I flip over, but the other side of the mattress is empty, the sheets mussed. I touch it, find the sheet cold. I peer at the clock, and can't believe it's ten in the morning. Good God, I never sleep in this late, and I have to be to work at noon. Must be this fresh seaside air making me groggy, and Sean's body wrapped around me, protecting me from monsters like raccoons in the garbage can. I listen for sounds of hammering on the roof, but none reaches my ears.

I push the blankets off and reach for my robe, my body still sore from yesterday's outdoor sex followed by a hot session in the shower. A quiver moves through me at the erotic memories. Honest to God, I still can't believe I did that. But Sean is becoming an addiction that I can't quit. I walk quietly down the hall and I find him in the kitchen preparing breakfast. I go still, wanting nothing more than to spend the rest of the morning admiring him unobserved.

My gaze travels over his back, the way his T-shirt pulls tight and stretches over his muscles as he moves. I inspect his jeans, the crazy way they hug his perfect ass. The things this man does to me without even trying are catastrophic and I want him again. I know getting in deeper with him isn't smart or rational, but since running away from my ex, very few of my actions have "brilliant" and "sensible" written all over them.

As if sensing my eyes on him, he turns slowly, spatula in hand.

"You're up."

"Can't get anything by you," I tease, and wonder what else might be *up* on this beautiful Monday morning.

My gaze instantly drops to his crotch before I can stop myself. I linger for a moment, admire the bulge in his jeans. Sean makes a sound and I quickly jerk my head up and meet his gaze. That all-knowing grin spreads across his face. God, how freaking embarrassing to be caught blatantly checking him out.

"Have you been awake long?" I ask, and pad across the floor to the kitchen island.

He points his spatula at something. "Long enough." I follow the direction, and when I see a grande Starbucks cup, my head comes back in surprise. "Did you—"

He turns his back to me to tend to the stove. "Yeah."

"Sean, that was so sweet of you."

"I had to go into Hope Falls." Broad shoulders shrug. "It's no big deal."

"Not to you but it is to me. Is it an Americano?"

He nods. "You'll have to warm it up. It's been sitting there for an hour."

I can't believe he remembered what I liked. I'm so . . . touched. "You are so sweet," I say again.

"I've been called a lot of things, and 'sweet' was never one of them."

"Well, you are."

He turns, and holds up the spatula, his eyes dark as they rake over me. "You want me to come over there and show you just how 'not sweet' I am?" I can't say I don't like his idea.

"Maybe."

"Jesus, girl." He points to the stool at the island. "Sit."

"Bossy much?"

"Sit," he says again and scowls at me.

"Fine, I'll sit. Let me heat this up first." I hurry to the microwave and warm up my coffee. He stands close beside me and I revel in his warmth and familiarity. The microwave beeps and I reach for my drink, open the lid, take a much needed sip. I let loose a low slow moan, much like the way Sean had made me moan yesterday. "Oh my God. Sean, that is so good." His body goes stiff. "What? Did I say something wrong?"

"You make those same moans when I'm inside you." He raises a brow. "Is the coffee really that good?"

"Up until that night at Dick's I'd say an Americano was *better* than sex," I admit.

He rubs the scruff on his chin, his eyes darker. "And now?"

"Not so much." He nods like that pleases him and I breathe in the delicious scents filling the kitchen as I finger comb my hair in some feeble effort to make myself presentable. "What smells so good?"

"Bacon."

He is a man of little words today. What's going on inside the busy brain of his? "Where did you get it? I didn't pick up any bacon."

"Butcher in Hope Falls. Best bacon around, and believe me, I've been around."

I crinkle my nose and wiggle until I'm comfortable on the island stool. "You went all the way to Hope Falls for bacon?"

"Yeah."

"Oh, I thought it had something to do with work."

"No."

I study the rigid way he moves and take in the stiffness in his back as he slides a plate of bacon, eggs, and toast across the counter. I want to get in there, help him work out the kink, but I can't give too much of myself away.

"Gotta love a man who can cook." *Love? Oh, God, don't give him the wrong idea, Summer.* "I mean—"

"Eat," he says and slides in beside me with his own plate. His jean-clad thigh lightly brushes mine as he sits. A quiver races through me, awakening all my senses. Honest to God, how can a nonsensual touch feel so sensual? Then again this is Sean I'm talking about. Everything with him feels sensual, even eating breakfast.

Having him in my bed last night was sensual, even though he hadn't touched me sexually. Instead every sweep of his hand, every tug of my body was soothing, comforting, just what I needed. How is it after all these years this man still knows what I need—and when I need it—much like when we were kids?

My mind trips back. Sometimes I couldn't see him, but always felt him in the background when we were young. He was there to give mouth-to-mouth the day I nearly drowned. He'd used the spare change in his pocket to replace the ice cream that had fallen from my cone, and that day when one of the boys in the cottage just down the road from mine started taunting me about my beginner's bra, Sean was there to give him a beating. That didn't go over too well with the vacationers, or the law. That night my mother drove home the fact that I needed to stay clear of the Owens boys. She never knew he was protecting me—the same way he always protected his brothers and cousins. I didn't dare defend him, for fear that Mom and Dad would keep me from Blue Bay. After Mom died though, everything had changed. I changed. While Sean might still be that protective boy from my youth, he's changed, too. There is something dark inside him. Living, breathing, brewing just below the surface. I see it when he doesn't know I'm looking.

I toss a piece of bacon into my mouth and my eyes go wide. "You weren't kidding, this is delicious."

"Double smoked and cut thick," he says. "That's why it's so good."

I grab another piece and chew. "I don't normally even eat breakfast."

"No."

"Nope." I lift my Starbucks. "Just coffee. If I eat like this every day I'll be a whale."

He turns slowly, his heated gaze raking over my curves. I feel it everywhere, and it makes my body burn hotter. "While I'm staying here, you'll be eating breakfast." His voice is low, quiet, almost unrecognizable

I spin on my chair. "Staying here?"

"Yeah." He turns from me, digs into his eggs and takes a big bite, but his breathing is a little uneven.

"Sean."

"What?"

"I don't need you to stay here. Last night I just got spooked."

He glares at me. "I'm staying."

"I don't—"

"You can keep your secrets," he warns his voice hard, unwavering. "But I'm staying."

I open my mouth to protest, but in a move that takes my

completely by surprise, he stands over me, pressing my back into the counter, his hands on either side of me. His eyes are dark, dangerous, his body sleek and solid. I let out a fluttery breath. He might be a warrior, but I feel so insulated in his arms, like nothing or no one can get to me.

"If you keep protesting, I'm going to put something in this mouth to stop you." I shiver at his dirty words as they trigger a flashback to last night, to when he said he needed his cock in my mouth. Lust hits like a triple shot of tequila. Dizzy with need, my breath catches, and I part my lips. A flick of my tongue moistens my mouth, a confession that I want that, too.

"Jesus, fuck," he whispers, and rakes his thumb over my mouth, rough, hard—a move that has ownership all over it. Flames spark inside me, my body responding to the need in his eyes. He pushes his thumb into my mouth and I suck hard. My sex clenches and the heat in my body spreads onward and outward.

"You want that?" he asks, the intensity in the way he's looking at me burns through me, and settles deep between my quivering legs.

"Yes."

"You want my cum in here." He moves his finger inside my mouth, swirling it around my tongue.

I nod, and suck him hard, wanting everything he has to give me. His nostrils flare, the green in his eyes deeper, a wild animal stalking the dark night, hunting its prey. He's going to claim me, I can barely breathe with excitement.

His hands go to my shoulder and he pushes down. "On your knees," he demands.

Without question, I drop to the floor, and he grips my hair as I rip into his jeans. Limbs shaking, I free his magnificent cock.

"See what you do to me," he murmurs.

I nod, loving that I can do this to him. I touch him and my hands looks so small and delicate on his shaft, feel cool as I stroke his long, hot length. I lean forward and his beautiful cock fattens before my eyes as I lick the throbbing tip. His hands rasp my shoulder as he jerks forward and nudges my mouth, demanding entrance.

God, he tastes good. Sweet and tangy, distinctly male and I want more. As my whole world becomes his cock, I run my tongue over his shaft, lick his crown, then widen my mouth to take him in.

"That's it," he groans, his voice tight. "Take me deep."

I rock forward until I can't breathe, but I don't care about that either. I want to hear his growls, his moans, want to have him shoot his cum down my throat. I want to eat him, drink him in, stay between his legs like this forever.

"Baby, I can't wait to get my mouth on your sweet pussy again." He groans and I record the sound to play it over and over in my head later, loving the way it vibrates through me. I pulse with a need so scary my heartbeat speeds up. "I'm going to put my tongue on you, suck your clit." He pauses to groan, then says. "Want to know what I'm going to do with my fingers?"

"Yes," I manage to say around a mouthful of fat cock.

He holds my head, takes charge of the speed and depths, fully controlling my movements. "After I get you hot and wet with my mouth, I'm going to slide them in to you. Two, maybe three. However many it takes to fill you. Then I'm going to finger fuck you so hard and deep, you're going to lose complete control." A hot rush spreads through me at his dirty, explicit words, and I love it. I love it so much I sink into a haze of sensations where nothing matters but this man, and the things he makes me feel. "You'll be so well fucked, you'll be lucky if you can even walk at work today. But that's okay. I fucking want every dickless asshole to know you're off limits.

You're mine and I plan to make sure everyone knows it." My pulse beats double time as my arousal flashes. He pants harder and rocks his hips, pushing his cock deeper into my throat. I've never taken a man so deep, never wanted to. Truthfully up until now, oral sex was a chore, not something I craved. But damn, I like taking Sean into my mouth, love his grunts, his dirty words as I take him to a different place where nothing exists but pleasure.

"You want that don't you, baby? You want every guy to know you're mine?" I nod, and make a whimpering sound. "Good." I steal a glance at him, take in his half-lidded eyes, the way his body is shaking. He's so close to the point of no return. "When you come for me, and baby, you're going to come so fucking hard and thorough, I'm going to lick every drop, until I taste nothing but you for the rest of the day. When the taste is gone tomorrow, I'm going to do it all over again."

I moan, and my pussy is so wet, my juices are dripping down my thigh. I glance up at him, and when I catch the way he's looking at me I gasp. No man has ever looked at me in the possessive way Sean is looking at me now. No wonder it's so easy to put myself in his hands. I tremble with the things I'm not supposed to be feeling for this man.

Harder and faster I work my mouth over him, a pace that has him tugging at my hair and jerking his hips wildly. Shameless want rockets through me and I shift my body, needing something, anything to take the edge off.

"Look at you. So needy for my cock." He brushes my hair back. "Touch yourself for me. Put your hands between your legs and stroke your clit."

I do as asked, desperate for release. I stroke my clit and gasp when sensations shoot through me. I've never been turned on from sucking cock before, but this is Sean and all he has to do is look at me the right way—or the wrong way—

and I'm well on my way to an orgasm. Truthfully, sex with this man is insane.

"That's it," he growls, his voice raspy as I lap at the tang of his excitement pooling on the end of his crown.

"I'm going to take you so hard, baby. Actually I might bend you over this counter and pound into your sweet pussy." A grunt and then, "Or maybe I'll lift this little nightie and expose your sweet ass." A quiver moves through me and his cock jumps in my mouth, a telltale sign how much he likes the idea of that. "Yeah, maybe I'll put my cock in that virgin hole of yours." I expel a low moan built of sexual frustration, and Sean tightens. "I think you like the idea of that."

Oh God, he has no idea, but he's too big, too thick. He'll ruin me. But there is some part of me that wants him to ruin me, to use and abuse me, own me completely. With those filthy thoughts urging me on, I lick the underside of his cock, then go lower to give his balls attention. As I suck, I stroke my clit harder, and my pussy squeezes, desperate for something to clench on to.

He thrusts into my mouth, and I lose my footing. He tightens his hand on my head, anchoring me so I don't fall. "I've got you," he whispers, and my heart squeezes. We both might be lost in a haze of lust, but he's always looking out for my well-being. A bolt of need zing through me, my body so close to shattering as his wet cock slides between my lips. My jaw aches from his girth, but I don't care. I want him in my mouth. I want him to shoot his cum down my throat. I want so much. Too much.

"Feel me? Feel me thicken," he asks, and holds my head still. I press my tongue to his veins, and he grunts. "I'm there. Fuck, baby, I'm going to come," he says, and powers forward until he hits the back of my throat. "I'm going to fill your mouth." His cock pulses, and a second later he's pumping into me. His taste swirls around me, and I swallow him. My throat works as I gulp, unable to take it all, and a little bit dribbles down my chin. Sean's groan grows louder when he sees it.

"You are so sexy," he whispers, his words are like a caress deep inside me. The world slows as my body clenches hard, the powerful vibrations pulling a gasp from my lungs. I struggle to breathe as my body throbs and tightens, heat jolting through me as I climax.

Sean touches my chin, lifts my face, and I'm so lost in pleasure I can't focus on him. I run my finger over my slick wetness, and my body jerks, as I come and come and come. He pulls his cock from my mouth, and I'm still forming an "O" as he bend to capture me in his arms, his harsh breaths falling over me. I'm shaking and barely able to fill my lungs as he lifts me, his cock pushing against my throbbing sex.

He presses his mouth to mine, and kisses me deeply as one hand trails lower, dips between my sopping wet thighs. "Jesus," he hisses, and plunges inside. "You're still coming." He works me hard, a rough massage brutal in its precision. His fingers showing no mercy as he grinds his palm on my clit. I keep exploding until I splinter into a million tiny pieces. Time seems to speed up, but then comes to a standstill as my body rocks and vibrates then comes back down to earth. Intense green eyes that are unrecognizable gaze at me with dark desire. Raw, primal—volatile—an erupting volcano, a brushfire tearing through the hillsides. Unstoppable. It shakes through me and I fight to catch my breath.

"I need to taste you," he says, and I don't even recognize his voice. "Then I'm going to bend you over this counter," he explains, the calmness in his tone belying the storm in his eyes. I grip his shoulders to hang on, unable to do anything else but bend to his will. He's about to slide down my body when someone knocks on the door.

"Fuck," Sean murmurs, but the sound seems to snap him back to this reality.

I freeze on boneless legs, and struggle to get my brain working. Who could be at my door? I look at Sean and there's no hiding the panic in my eyes.

His jaw clenches. "It's my brother," he says quickly. He puts his hands on my shoulders and absorbs my tremor. His eyes have sobered, but I can still see the lust, the embers needing only a spark to fire them. "It's okay." One big strong hand closes over my cheek and he dips his head. Concern reflects in his eyes. "I asked him to come. He's here to install a security system. Nothing to be worried about."

"I . . . I can't afford that, Sean."

"Don't worry about it."

"Sean . . ." I begin but then shut my mouth. I might as well be arguing with a goldfish. When Sean sets his mind to something there is no stopping him. He was like that as a kid, and apparently that hasn't changed over the years.

"I'm not done with you." He grips my chin, and looks at my lips. I wipe my hand over my wet mouth, and work to regulate my breathing. "What time is your break today?"

"I have the lunch crowd at noon, but it should die off around two. I'll probably take my break after that."

"We're going to finish what we started."

He's going to come to my work? "Sean, I can't—"

"Oh, yeah, you can. And we will."

He zips up his pants, and gives me a slap on the ass. "Finish your breakfast. I'll let Jamie in."

I should run to my room to put more clothes on, but I sit back down, not sure my legs will actually work. I need a minute, or two, or a million to get myself together and process. My glance drops to Sean's ass as he saunters to the door like we hadn't just been having sex. Unlike him, I'm not as quick to recover. I try to fix my hair, to present normal, but I have sex written all over me and there is no hiding that. He lets Jamie in—another one of the Owens brothers who thinks he knows me. He's right. He does. He was always tight on Sean's heels when they were young. On that note, I stand. I'd better get a move on it before he starts asking questions again. I toss the rest of the bacon into my mouth, say a quick hello to Jamie, and hurry to the shower.

I wash quickly, my body still humming from my delicious morning wake-up sex—it was way better than the bacon and the Americano. Yes I want more, too, but no way am I going to have sex with Sean at Winchesters. I need this job. The money in the lockbox is only going to go so far and I don't dare go to the bank. Jack could be tracking my transactions.

I dress in my jeans, pull on my black work shirt with "Winchesters" emblazoned across the back, and grab my apron. I step into the room to find Sean still talking to Jamie, and pointing out areas where he'd like motion detectors installed. I stare for a moment, my heart squeezing at their brotherly camaraderie. The Owens brothers might not have seen each other for years, but they're tight, a brotherhood that nothing can come between. I breathe past the longing. I'd always wanted siblings, wanted to grow up in a big family like Sean's, but it wasn't in the cards for me. That doesn't mean I don't want it now, though. I used to have girlish dreams of walking down the aisle, my dad giving me away. I'd wanted a big wedding, just like I wanted a big family. Now, well I'm not so sure I'll ever have that. I put my hand in my pocket, feel for the key that opens God knows what, and strive to fight down the tension inside me.

Sean's gaze slowly turns to me, burns through my body like a lit match when our eyes meet. He steps up to me, and despite our audience of one, drops a slow, lingering kiss full of dirty promises onto my mouth. I stand there, lips parted gazing at him like he's a god long after he breaks the kiss. He puts his lips to my ear. "See you soon."

"Okay," I say breathlessly. I hurry to my truck, climb in, and make my way to work. As I drive the short distance to town, I see kids are on their bicycles riding circles around each other, some are at the outside eating ice cream, and a group of women are all standing around on the sidewalk chatting while their kids skip rope and play. My heart warms at the sight. I really do love this small town.

I pass by the post office again. After work I'll stop in, see if the key opens something. Then again, maybe it's a key to a safe-deposit box at the bank. Or it could open something at the bus station. Perhaps it could be to a locker there, or in the town's fitness center. I'd been gathering information of all the possible places the key might work, and now that I've settled in, I can start checking them out.

I tap the brakes as I pull into the lot at Winchesters and steal a quick glance around before slipping from the cab. My feet hit the ground with a slap. God, I'll never get used to driving this beast of a vehicle. I hurry inside and run in to Stacey in the back room. The other night when Tyler and Jamie were fighting on the floor, she'd warned me about the Owens brothers, told me not to get involved. From the way Sean was watching us, I get the feeling he knew exactly what she was saying to me. According to her they are all players. Not one single Owens boy is out for anything other than a good time. Of course, I found out later she'd been involved with Jacob, one of the twins, and he skipped town the night they were to go to the prom. But it did make me wonder about the girls who were all over the guys the other night. The Owens brothers attract girls like dimwitted moths to a lightbulb.

Do any one of them have what it takes to be faithful, a one-woman kind of man?

I quickly shut down my thoughts and tie my apron around my waist. I'm having sex with Sean, incredible, mind-blowing sex for sure, but I'm not planning to stay here. I have a career to get back to, a practice I built from the ground up, and who knows what his plans are after he gets his father's business up and running. There's no saying he doesn't hit the circuit again and hand the reins to any one of the other guys.

I hurry into the pub, and come across a group of grand-mothers, all wearing red hats. I pull my notepad from my pocket, ready to forget about Sean for a while, but when one of the women smiles at me, and I see the distinct color of her eyes and my heart misses a beat.

Grandma Nellie.

"What can I get for you ladies?" I ask, and try not to react. I remember her from years ago. She was always so sweet and kind to me. She and my mom would talk in the center of town, and while Mom liked her it still didn't change the fact that she wanted me nowhere near her grandsons.

Nellie zeroes in on my nametag. "Well I'm thinking you're the girl who has my grandson all tied up in knots."

I have Sean all tied up in knots?

My pulse jumps in my throat. That can't be right.

"I'm afraid that's not on the menu," I tease hoping to change the subject.

She laughs and winks at me. "Beautiful and smart." She looks around the table. "My boys have good taste," she says and they all nod in agreement. Astute eyes zero back in on me, go serious. "Did he mention Sunday dinner?"

"No . . . I . . . uh . . ."

"That's just like Sean." She looks heavenward and rolls her eyes. "Can't keep a single thought around a pretty girl. Anyway, dinner is this Sunday. Six sharp."

"I don't—"

She waves a dismissive hand. "That's right, you don't need

to bring anything. Just show up." Good God, she's as pushy as Sean. Now I know where he gets it. But no way am I going there for Sunday dinner. It's not like Sean and I are dating.

"I don't think—"

"How is the Cobb salad?" one of the other women asks.

I turn to her. "Wait, uh . . ."

"That looks good, Mary," one of the other ladies says as she removes her big hat and sets it down beside her. They all close their menus.

"Cobb salads, all around," someone else pipes in.

I blink, and try to get back on track. "I . . . uh . . ."

"See you Sunday, dear," Grandma Nellie says and they all shoo me away. I walk toward the kitchen to put the order in, my brain racing a million miles an hour.

What the hell just happened?

SUMMER

I don't need to turn to know Sean has entered the restaurant and has pinned with me those turbulent green eyes of his. I feel him long before I see him. Every nerve in my body jumps, comes alive under his dark stare.

As need sings through my veins, I strive to make my legs work and carry the bowls of pasta to my last table. I try to ignore all six feet of him standing there, oozing testosterone that is messing with the greedy spot between my legs, but that would be like standing in the middle of a highway and pretending an eighteen wheeler wasn't about to mow me down. I turn, unable to help myself, and catch him staring.

My insides tighten. What is it about a guy in jeans and work boots that gets to me? Correction. What is it about Sean in jeans and work boots that gets to me? His brothers are dressed the same, but I only see Sean.

"I'm not done with you."

As his parting words dance around inside my brain, my entire body quakes, but no way, no how can we finish what we started here at the bar. His brothers stop to talk to Beck, and when Sean lowers that big hard body into one of the wooden chairs in the corner, I figure it's as good a time as any to talk to him about his grandmother's visit. I'm sure he'll make this right so I don't have to go. Deep down I don't want to go. Not one little bit.

Okay, maybe a tiny little bit—or a lot.

But I can't go there with Sean. I can't get involved with him like that. He's not asking for more and I have trouble nipping at my heels.

As I approach his table, I see a Starbucks cup in his hands. My steps slow. Seriously, he went to Starbucks? I sure could use an Americano right about now, but surely to God, he didn't make a run to Hope Falls to get me another one. That would be . . . too sweet.

"Hey," I say as I approach.

"Hey yourself." He holds the coffee out to me, and my heart squeezes. "You rushed out this morning before your finished your coffee, so I thought you could use another one. This one should still be warm."

I swallow against the tightness in my throat as my pulse beats double time against my neck. I could get used to this, used to Sean. But we're simply playing house, and I can't forget that. "You didn't have to do that."

"Didn't have to. Wanted to." He gives me that familiar shrug again. "Besides I was in Hope Falls."

"Bacon?" I tease in an effort to uncoil the knot in my gut.

He laughs. "For work actually. Needed some supplies." He looks at his brothers and scowls. "My brother Tyler is working on a project, adding a new addition to one of the oceanfront homes, not too far from yours actually."

"And that's a problem why?"

"What? I never said that was a problem"

"You're scowling. You scowl when something is pissing you off." His scowl deepens and I grin. "Yeah, that's it. Just like that. That's what I'm talking about."

"I do not scowl."

"Yeah, you do, and you glare, too." I laugh as he continues to glare at me, a scowl marring his handsome features. I straighten. "Wait. Am I pissing you off now?"

"Yeah, you're pissing me off. I don't scowl or glare."

"Need a mirror?" He growls as I pull the tab back on the coffee cup lid and take a sip. "Mmmm," I moan. Lust replaces his glare and his eyes drop to my mouth. "Sorry," I say quickly and make a mental note to quit moaning every time I drink a coffee. At least when we're in public and we can't do something about it. But the look in his eyes warns he doesn't care if we have an audience.

On that note, I put on my best professional face and say, "What can I get you?"

"Do you even have to ask?" he grumbles.

Before I can answer, his brothers and Beck all grab a seat at the table. I take their orders, the whole time Sean's eyes ablaze with lust, and go to the back to punch them in. I hurry through my shift, and about a half hour later I turn back to see Sean by himself.

The guys are all gone, and I catch him unguarded as he stares at his glass of soda, like it holds all the answers to the universe. I take in the quiet reflective side of him. What is going through that mind of his? The last of my customers slide from their booth, and the only ones left in the pub is the kitchen staff, a couple of the other waitresses, and Sean. He's nursing his soda, looking like he's a million miles away, fighting demons that no one can see but him.

The door kicks shut as the last of the diners leave, and it jolts Sean back to the present. His gaze scans the pub, locks on mine, and that dark, contemplative looks softens when our gazes collide. A dangerous grin tugs at the corners of his mouth, and the gleam in his eyes worries me. I practically vibrate beneath his stare. Oh, God, I am in so much trouble.

He pushes from the chair and I turn my back to him, walk up to the bar, and go over my receipts. His boots pound on the floor, keeping rhythm with my crashing heart as he cages me, and his scent curls around me like a powerful aphrodisiac.

"Busy," he asks, his nearness making me breathless.

"Very."

His hand touches the back of my neck, trails lower, leaving goose bumps in its wake. "No time for a break."

"Actually there is something I want to talk to you about."

He stands solidly behind me. "What I want to do to you involves my mouth, too," he says his voice teasing, playful and I admit I love this side of him. In fact I love all sides of him. I take a breath to battle my desires, when all I want to do is surrender myself to him. But his grandmother was here, and we can't let her go around thinking we're a couple. We're not.

"Your grandmother," I begin.

He stiffens. "What about her?"

"She was here today."

"And?"

I spin to see him and I know it's cliché but good God, he is so beautiful he takes my breath way. "She invited me to Sunday dinner."

He shakes his head. "Fucking Tyler."

"Tyler?"

"Yeah, he told Gram I had a thing for you."

"A thing?" I jump to the worst conclusion, as always. "He didn't tell her we were . . ."

"No he didn't tell her we were fucking." His thumb goes to my mouth and he brushes it over my bottom lip, rough, greedy. Jesus, he's going to devour me. "I told her we were just friends, but Gram would like nothing better than to see me settled down." A noise crawls out of his throat, a scoff of sorts. I can only imagine it means it will be cold day in hell before he settles down. Guess Stacey was right. The Owens boys aren't marriage material. Not that I'm looking for anything that resembles a white wedding from Sean.

"Can you get me out of it?" I ask. "We're not dating and I don't want to give your grandmother the wrong idea."

His brow pulls together, a flash of disappointment on his face, then he wipes it away as fast as it appeared. What the hell? Does he want me to go? Honest to God, he's strong and steady, tough and rough, but a contradiction to me in so many ways.

"Not going to happen." He clicks his tongue. "Gram gets what Gram wants."

I poke him in the chest. "Like someone else I know," I say as he drags his finger down my throat, like he's anxious to explore my body again.

God, I want that, too.

"No changing her mind, unless you want a hell of a fight on your hands. She's not above causing a scene either."

Nervousness steals over me. "I prefer to keep a low profile."

"Looks like you're going to have to *come* then."

Why is it I feel like he's talking about something else entirely now. The dirty grin on his face? Possibly. The way he's rubbing his hard cock against me and putting emphasis on the word "come"? Definitely. He lifts his gaze, does a sweep of the room, then grabs my hand.

"Come with me."

"Where are we going?" I ask on a breathless whisper, not that I care anymore. I'm pretty sure I'd follow him into the depths of hell right now, if it meant he was going to touch me again. Damn my mutinous body. So much for my resolve to keep my distance at work . . . or my distance from him at all.

I'm not done with you.

I don't even want to think about the mess I'm going to be in when he *is* done with me. He opens the storage room, drags me in and closes the door, plunging us in darkness.

"Sean," I whisper, a giggle catching in my throat as something strange comes over me. Honest to God, I feel like I'm thirteen again, playing seven minutes in heaven with some slobbering boy at a friend's first teenage birthday party. Except Sean is not some slobbering kid who has no idea how to kiss. No, his kisses are like magic. The second our lips touch, poof, my panties always seem to disappear.

"Something funny?" His deep voice sizzles through me.

"No, it's just that the last time I was in a dark closet it was with Danny Fitzgerald."

His muscles are tight beneath my hand. "Who the fuck is Danny Fitzgerald?"

"I was at my first boy-girl party and we were playing seven minutes in heaven."

He relaxes a bit, slips his hand around my body and grips my ass. I yelp. "Seven minutes, huh?"

"What, you've never played?"

My hands race over him with aroused eagerness and electricity arcs between us. I wouldn't be surprised if the room suddenly lights up.

"I've played plenty," he says, "But with you seven minutes will never be enough."

I open my mouth to say something but he swallows my reply as his lips come down over mine. I moan and sag into him. He kisses me deep, hard, and desire slams in to me. My limbs weaken as his tongue plays with mine, and leaves me hot, needy . . . wordless. Jesus the man kisses like this is no game.

His hands slide under my shirt. "All day these have been on my mind." He tugs my bra down, and my body ignites when his hot mouth closes over one nipple. I cry out and his other hand goes over my mouth to stifle it. I giggle a little, feeling reckless, and carefree, like I'm twelve again and the boy of my dreams is giving me mouth-to-mouth down by the shore. He tugs my nipples between his teeth and gently bites down. I arch into him and moan.

"That feels so good."

And I am so not twelve again.

His lips abandon my breasts and he unbuttons my jeans and has them around my ankles before I even realize what's going on. Damned if he isn't a man of many talents. I rub up against him, needing the contact. He slides a hand into my panties, and sinks a finger into me. Slick, easy strokes that have me panting in record time.

"Yeah, that's it. Nice and wet for me just like I knew you'd be."

Talented fingers light me up, and I clamp my legs together to ride him. His mouth finds mine again and tongues join and tangle as he drives another finger inside. I gulp, control a thing of the past as I take what I need. I tear my mouth away, and throw my head back, nothing mattering but what he's doing between my legs.

He sinks to his knees, and presses his mouth to my clit. He sucks on it so hard, sensations rip through me and steal the air from my lungs. I want his cock in me so badly I ache deep in my core. I tremble, pant, share in his urgency, and when he applies more pressure, I let go and come around his fingers.

"Fuck yes," he murmurs and laps at me. "I've been thinking about this all day, too." He stays between my legs and my erotic whimpers fill the room, but I need more.

"Sean, please." I pull him to me and he stands. Need burns

in my throat as he presses against me. "Inside me . . . now . . . hurry . . ."

His needy curses coil around me as he unzips his pants, turns me around and bends me over one of the shelving units. With my jeans to my knees his thick head nudges my opening from behind and I rear back forcing him in.

"Fuck me," he growls.

"No, fuck me." Good Lord he's turning me into a freaking addict with a mouth as dirty as his. He drives his entire length into me.

"Oh, my God," I cry out, but it only fuels him. He pumps, slams, thrusts like a man hell bent on taking what's his. He fists my hair and shivers of need race through me. I cry out, a keening sound that I try to muffle with my hands.

I push back, wanting him deeper, harder, unable to get enough. His hand presses on my back to still me, and my blood pulses so hot, I'm afraid I might go up in a burst of flames.

Rippling waves of an orgasm take hold and my breath comes in a jagged burst. I cry out in ecstasy, as wet warmth pools between my legs.

"I feel you," he murmurs. "So slick and hot on my cock."

He rams hard and I meet and welcome his racing strokes, as he bangs me against the shelving, his severe, blunt thrusts create heat and friction until I'm lost, delirious with desire. I gasp as another hot, hard orgasm ambushes me, and I bite my lip to stifle a cry, as some working brain cell reminds me where I am.

"Sean," I murmur and he lifts my shirt and puts his mouth on my back. He presses hot kisses, his hands gripping my hips as he pumps, his heart pounding against my back as he leans over me. I can taste the tension in the air, expanding, filling every corner, until an explosion is inevitable. He straightens and drives hard. I steal a glance at him over my shoulder, take in the savage look on his face, fierce, predatory, possessive, a desperate sort of need in his eyes as they connect with mine. My heart hammers and I swallow against the thickness in my throat.

"Summer," he whispers, or at least I think that's what he called me, but I'm so far gone, lost in him, my heart pounding so hard I my ears, I can't hear right. He throws his head back, his hands biting into my hips, bruising delicate flesh, and let's himself go, pumping his seed high inside me. I squeeze around him, keeping his cum in me, not wanting to lose a single drop.

Gasping hard, we both stay still, motionless for a long time, then he runs his hand along my back, grips my shoulder and lifts me until my back is against his powerful chest.

His mouth goes to my ear. "You're incredible."

"That was . . ." I can quite put into words what that was.

"Fun?"

My heart sinks a little. Yes, it was fun, but it felt like so much more. It felt like his kisses were real, like there was something more going on between us. Like we crossed an imaginary line there is no coming back from.

Someone walks by the door, we see a shadow under the bottom crack and Sean shifts his body to block mine in case it opens. When the footsteps become distant, he tugs my panties and jeans back up, and fixes my bra and shirt.

His lips find mine, a soft kiss, so full of tenderness and emotions I'm having a hard time wrapping my brain around the two of us, and this sex only relationship. His zipper cuts through the quiet as he fixes himself.

"All set," he whispers, his hand going around my neck to cup it. His thumb brushes lightly, and my heart squeezes.

"Yeah," I say, trying to keep my voice light.

Sean cracks the door and when he finds the coast clear, he ushers me out. I fix my hair as I walk down the hall and try to pull of casual, even though I have Sean's scent all over me and vice versa. One look at us, and it's easy to tell what we were doing in that back room. Fortunately the restaurant is empty when we emerge and my boss Beck had left with the other two Owens brothers earlier.

We reach the bar and he casts me a grin and says, "See you at home tonight."

My heart flips and I swallow down the lump punching into my throat. I shouldn't like the sound of that so much, the idea that going home to him every night is something I could so easily get used to. Falling in bed together every night would be the nicest thing, but more importantly waking up with him every morning would be even better. But we're just playing house, exploring a brief affair while I'm here, and I'd be wise to remember that.

"See you later," I say and inject a lightness into my voice.

He stops, cups my elbow, and draws me close. Green eyes darken as they move over my face, and my lids flutter. "Everything okay?"

Why is it I can never get anything by this man? "Perfect. I just need to get back to work," I say.

He peruses the empty pub, a dubious look on his face, but instead of calling me on it, he says, "Okay." His gaze returns to mine. "How about I grab us a pizza for dinner?"

"Pizza is perfect." I brace myself against the bar, needing it for support as I watch him saunter out. When the door bangs shut behind him I draw a quick breath and remind myself what's real and what isn't. Sex is for fun, nothing else. With that last thought in mind, I go over my receipts again.

The rest of my shift flies by in a blur and I clock out at four. I untie my apron, and shove it into my purse. Instead of going to my truck, I hurry down the sidewalk still filled with kids playing, and enter the post office. I stand in line, two people ahead of me as the man behind the counter searches for a parcel. He's as old as Benny, and should have retired years ago. Must be the fresh county air that keeps these folks going.

Close to fifteen minutes later, I'm at the counter, but when the bell over the door jingles and a shiver moves down my spine I don't need to turn to know Sean has entered. His boots scrape and the next thing I know his mouth is near my ear.

"Come here often?"

I turn and try to make light of the situation. "Real original." He flashes that ridiculously sexy dimple. "You could have come up with something better like, 'Excuse me, were you checking out my package?'"

With that Sean laughs, and the sound goes right through me. The elderly gentleman behind the counter, however, finds nothing funny about the situation.

"Can I help you?" he says again, and I hesitate. Shoot, I want to ask about the key but don't want to raise Sean's suspicions. He already knows I'm a keeping a secret, or two, and that I'm pretending to be someone I'm not.

"I . . . uh . . . found this key, and was just wondering if belonged to a post office box."

The elderly gentleman lifts his head and looks through the lower part of his glasses. "Nope, not one of ours. You might want to try the bus station."

"Thanks," I say and shove it into my pocket. I plaster a smile on my face and turn, but Sean isn't smiling when I try to walk past him. He cups my elbow and pulls me against his hard body. There are other customers in the post office, and they're darting glances our way but Sean doesn't seem to worry about the attention we're drawing.

"What's up?" he asks.

"Oh, nothing." I lean forward, let my hair mask my

features. "I just found this at the house, thought someone might have lost it, or it belonged to the Wheeler family."

He stares at me for a long moment, long enough to make me uncomfortable, then let's me go. "I have a few more stops to make, then I'll meet you at home."

There he goes using that "home" word again.

I nod and leave the post office. Out on the busy sidewalk, I look up and down the street, unable to decide if I'm happy or not that I hadn't yet discovered the secrets this key will unlock. Wouldn't it be easier to just pretend it didn't exist, to live in ignorant bliss as I hide out here in Blue Bay for the rest of my life? But if Jack had something to do with Dad's death I plan to get to the bottom of it.

The warm sun beats down on me and I jump into my truck, make the trek home. I enter the cottage and breathe in. Unlike when I first arrived, everything smells clean and pure, like sunshine after a hard rain. I hear children laughing in the ocean just beyond my back door, and for the first time since I've been back, a sense of home washes over me. I'd forgotten how much I love it here. I breathe deep, let it out slowly and exhale all my fears. I'm not sure what's come over me, maybe it was the "kissing closet," the lightness Sean makes me feel. I briefly close my eyes and open them again, deciding to focus on the good memories from my past, the love I feel in every corner of the cottage. It almost feels like my parents have their arms around me, hugging me from above—protecting me from harm. Then again, maybe that's why the lockbox had a key to our cottage, to a place where I'd find Sean. He's only boy who's ever displayed protective-ness. Could my father have wanted this? Wanted me to find him? Or am I just really stretching things for my own benefit?

I step into the living room and as I walk to the back window to glance out over the ocean, I see Sean has already started tearing up the floors and there is a big hole in the wall where the water had been dripping.

The ocean beckons me and since Sean said he had to make another stop, I decide to go for a swim. I hurry to my room, pull on the one-piece bathing suit I'd picked up the other day and rush to the water. I swim out, but not too far. I don't dare. Sean isn't around to give me mouth-to-mouth should I need it.

I enjoy the cool water rushing around me, and as the dinner hour approaches, many of the families pack up their supplies and head home. Only a few sun worshippers remain, catching the last of the day's rays before the sun sets on the horizon. From the water I can see the back of the house, and I glance up to catch Sean coming my way. He has something in his arms, something big, but from where I am I can't tell what it is, although I do know it's not a pizza.

I push through the water and step onto the sand. I grab my towel, blot my face and wrap it around me. The second I see what Sean has in his arms, my heart beats wildly, and my lungs clench so tight, it hurts to breathe. He did this for me?

"Sean? What . . ."

He grins. "For you."

I look into his face, search his eyes and beneath the tough and rough surface, see the amazing, sweet man he really is. "You're kidding?"

"Nope.

I step up to him, and when I get close, I get a great big wet tongue across my face. Sean and I both laugh and he sets the playful retriever on the sand. The pup takes off, and darts into the water.

It barks and nips at the waves, and we both laugh, the last of the heaviness inside me taking flight. I take in the bright-ness in Sean's eyes and my heart soars. With so much weight around us lately, we needed this laugh.

"Why are you giving me a golden retriever pup?" I ask, but I already know the answer.

"Well," he says. "Since you're spooked at the cottage, I thought you might like to have a dog for company, or for when you're scared. If she's anything like Bear, she can chase off a raccoon, or . . . any other intruders."

"Bear?" I ask, even though I know the answer.

"Tyler's old dog," he says. "Summer used to love him."

I nod as my heart wobbles at his thoughtfulness. First a surveillance system and now this. I step up to him, press my cold wet body to his warmth. "I thought you were my guard dog."

The playfulness leaves his face. "I can't be there twenty-four seven. I have other jobs to check on, and well . . ." He brushes his thumb along my cheek and gestures toward the dog. "She's going to get big really fast."

My smile drops. "Sean," I begin. "I can't have dog. I don't know how long I'll be staying, and I only have a small condo back in SoCal. A retriever needs space to run and play."

"It's fine." He rolls one shoulder. "I'll take her when you're gone."

I eye him. "You're not planning to hit the motocross circuit again?"

"No, I gave that up." He clenches down on his jaw, those demons back in his eyes. "I have a responsibility here now." He looks past my shoulders. "Only one question remains."

"What's that?"

"What are you going to call her?"

I turn to see the pup playing and laugh. "Scout."

His brow pulls together. "Scout?"

"Yeah, from *To Kill a Mockingbird*."

"Really. Why?"

I roll one shoulder. "Because she's going to be tough and see the good in people."

His head dips and the corner of his mouth turns up. "Like you."

I lift my chin. "You think I'm tough and see the good in people?"

His knuckles brush mine and intense eyes study me darkly. "I think you're a lot of things."

"I think you're a lot of things, too, Sean."

"Don't say "sweet," otherwise I'll put you over my knee and slap that ass of yours."

"Okay, then. I think you're solid, dependable, a really great guy."

His face darkens, those demons he's running from clawing him out from the inside. My stomach tightens. I hate that look on him, would do just about anything to chase it away. Then again, I probably have that same look on my face. Aren't we the pair? Two messed up people who can't outrun the things hunting them.

"We should get back." He jerks his thumb over his shoulder. "Pizza is getting cold."

Needing to lighten things, I turn and say, "Here Scout." The puppy ignores me of course, so I run to the water and get her. Silence hangs heavy as we trek back to the cottage.

We step inside and the delicious scent of pepperoni and cheese hits me. My stomach grumbles. "I'm hungrier than I realized."

"Me, too, really worked up an appetite at work today."

I grin as my mind takes me back to the closet. "Me, too."

Sean grabs some plates as I play with Scout, but she's soon tuckered out from the excitement of the day and curls up in the bed Sean bought.

"Where did you get her?

"Friend of mine. He's a breeder. Very reputable. Sold me all this stuff to go with her." I take in the bag of food bigger than Sean, the toys, bowls, blankets, bed, leash, and at least a dozen other things. Sean rolls his eyes. "She's a pup, what does she need with all that stuff?"

"She won't be a pup for long though."

He hands me a slice of pizza and I bite into it. "Mmm," I moan.

"You know you really need to find another sound."

"You don't like it when I moan in the bedroom?"

"Yeah, I fucking do." He gazes at his cock and I follow the direction. "But outside the bedroom, my dick can't take it."

I laugh and point to his pizza. "Eat." I wink at him. "Maybe I'll see what I can do to help little Sean out later."

"Little?"

I laugh and bite into my pizza. "Eat."

Sean takes a big bite and I jump up and pour us each a soda. He takes a big swig and finishes off his slice in record time.

He reaches for another and winces as he pulls his arm back. "Son of a bitch," he says and rotates his shoulder.

"Still bothering you?"

"Yeah." His eyes darken, go playful. "I believe I do remember you saying something about working out the kink."

My mouth drops open and my eyes go wide. "Not in front of the puppy," I tease back.

He laughs and jerks his head toward the hall. "We could always take this into the other room."

"Actually, let me have a look at your shoulder first." I stand and move in behind him. I feel along his shoulder and down his back. He groans, but I'm pretty sure it's from pleasure, not pain. I lightly whack the side of his head. "Cut it out."

"What do you expect when you're touching me like this?" He grabs another slice and bites in to it as I work on him.

"Do you react like this whenever you're touched?"

He goes strangely quiet for a moment, then in a lower voice says, "No."

My body fires, because no one has the effect on me the way Sean does either, but as much as I'd love to take him in the bedroom, he needs something else from me. "Any chance you can lay on the floor for me?"

"Are you trying to have your way with me again?"

"Sean . . . ," I grumble

"Not that I mind but I think the bed would be softer."

I give him a warning glare, and he laughs and holds his hands up. "Okay, okay. The floor it is."

He walks into the living room, flattens himself on the boards that aren't damaged and puts his hands above his head. I drop down next to him, lift his arm and move it around to check the rotator cuff. "First of all, you have a damaged rotator cuff."

"Tell me something I don't know."

"How did it happen?"

"Fell off a damn bike. It was raining, and I took a hairpin turn too fast."

"Yikes."

He gives that easy shrug again. "I'm alive."

I feel along his back, and when I find the joint that is locked up, I go up on my knees and apply force. It pops back, and a loud snapping sound follows.

"Jesus, what are you doing to me?"

"You're a mess back here. Have you seen a doctor about this?"

"No, haven't had time."

"Well you're back in town now so I'd suggest you get this checked out."

"Isn't that what I'm doing?"

Instead of answering, I say, "Sean."

"Yeah."

"This afternoon, you were scowling about something. What was that all about?"

"Work stuff."

"What kind of work stuff?"

He pauses for a moment like he's not sure he wants to talk about it, then says, "I need to get a damn building permit, but Officer Walker is stalling things at city hall."

I run my hand along his vertebra checking the joints. "Why does he hate you?"

"He and Dad go way back. Dad stole his girl in high school, and married her afterward. I used to call her mom."

His mom had died shortly after we left Blue Bay for good, but I remember hearing Dad talk about it. It broke my heart, and I wanted so desperately to be here for him.

"I'm sorry about your mom."

"Thanks."

"Are your folks still alive?" he asks.

"No. I lost my mom years ago," I say and glance down that hallway. If he knows I'm Summer, and it's clear he does, he'd already knows what happened to my mother. But we're playing a game here, and I'm grateful he's playing along. "My dad, I lost him six months ago."

"I'm sorry." He turns, and the genuine sadness in his gaze brings water to my eyes. I miss my folks so much. Feeling lost, empty, a little twisted up inside I draw in a slow breath. Sean sits up, and presses his lips to mine. He kisses me with a savagery that tells me how lost he is, how he's hurting every bit as much as I am. As my gaze moves over his face, greed, hunger, and something dark and needy seems to take hold of him.

"Sean," I whisper as something potent, something I'm absolutely certain there is no coming back from pulses between us. Entirely lost in the moment, in him, I let go, forget that I'm not supposed to feel, because I need to feel. I need to feel Sean in my arms, bed, between my legs.

"Yeah?" His eyes are wild, needy. Fierce. He's never looked sexier.

"You said something about the bedroom."

11

SEAN

I'd been tearing up the floor for a solid day now, and thanks to Summer helping me work the kinks out every night, my shoulder is feeling a hell of a lot better. I hear the shower turn off and she's humming a tune as she pads to the bedroom to get dressed. I have to admit, I like when she's happy like this, carefree, if only for a few moments in the day. Outside, tied up in a shaded area to keep her safe from construction, Scout barks at the kids playing in the water. Sunshine slants in through the back window, and using my forearm, I wipe beads of sweat from my forehead. It's only midmorning and the cottage is already like a sauna. The forecast is calling for rain later, and I hope like hell it clears the humidity.

I set down the circular saw I'd been using and reach for the crowbar. One of the boards, swollen and water damaged is being a real bitch to get up. I slide the bar under it, give it a tug and it comes away in pieces. I toss the scraps aside and dig in with my bare hands to tear the rest away. I finally pull it from the subfloor, which looks pristine. At least the water hasn't destroyed the rough floorboards beneath the damaged oak. Costs won't be quite as high if we don't have to tear into the plywood. By my count, only half the wood floor needs to be removed. I can easily replace the boards, sand them down and stain them to match.

I kick a few boards with my boots, and I'm about to turn when something shiny catches my eye. I drop to my knees, and scrape at the golden circular object, which is jammed halfway under one of the good boards that I have no intention of removing. Whoever laid this floor did a shit job, with all the swelling and contracting from the changing seasons, it's no wonder something got lost. I free the shiny piece of jewelry and lay it in my palm to examine it.

"Whoa," I say and go back on my heels.

"Whoa what?" I hold the gold wedding band up for Summer to see and her big brown eyes go alarmingly wide, like she's seen a ghost. It's a small ring, wouldn't even fit on my pinkie. "I think it's a woman's wedding ring."

Summer goes so quiet I can practically hear her heart pound in her chest. She stares at the band like it's an apparition, and when I hold it out to her, her fingers ball and press into her stomach.

I stand and watch her carefully, waiting for some telltale sigh that this belongs to her mother. When she continues to stare, saying nothing I ask, "Do you think this belonged to the Wheelers?"

Standing unnaturally stiff, she nods, then those haunted brown eyes of hers slide to mine. I take in the pain, the little-girl-lost look on her face, and my lungs collapse.

"Jenna," I say, but she turns away, like she's only mildly interested. The act is lost on me. I see her raw pain. It falls over me like a physical blow. I want to pull her to me, tell her everything will be okay. But how can I tell her that when she won't open up to me—is pretending her mother's long lost ring means nothing to her. Anger flares hot inside me, but I tamp it down and curse myself. She's lost, scared, and hurting. Am I really going to act like an ass because she doesn't want to tell me what's going on in her life? For fuck's sake, that's not what she needs from me right now and hurting her in any way would destroy me

"Here," I say, and hand it to her. She curls her fingers around it, and holds it to her chest, but goddammit I want to be the thing she holds on to, the guy she turns to for comfort.

A long pause, and then, "Thank you," she says, her voice as cool and calm as she can make it, but I can see the rattled little girl beneath the surface. Every now and then she lets me glimpse her.

Her breathing changes, becomes harsher, and it's easy to tell she's fighting the tears. "Jenna."

"Yeah." She turns from me, and I get it. She doesn't want me to call her on it, doesn't want me to say a fucking word about who she really is.

"You'd better get to work. It's getting late."

"Okay," she says, her voice, soft, shaky as she grabs her apron off the back of the chair.

"Wait." Fuck man, I might be pissed that she refuses to open up to me but no way can I let her drive in her current state. "I have to run to town. Why don't you let me drive you?"

"It's—"

"Come on," I say, not giving her a choice. "I have a bunch of things to do so I'll be back and forth all day. It's no problem for me to pick you up either."

"Okay," she says and I'm surprised when she caves so easily. She likes to do everything herself, but even she knows she's in no state to drive. I'd suggest she take the day off but I'm not going to push my luck. I untie Scout from outback and Summer gives her a hug and kiss before she kennels her safely inside.

We jump in the truck and she's quiet, lost in her own thoughts as I drive. I slide my hand across the seat and capture hers. She gives me a weak smile and I feel like shit, wishing I could do something to help her. But fuck, how can I do that when she's still not being honest with me. This shit is really starting to piss me off.

I finally pull up to Winchesters. "What time are you off?"

"I finish at five."

"I'm going to do my best to get the floor finished today. Then all that's left is to fix the wall." A tight knot forms at the thoughts of finishing the job, walking away from Summer.

"Thanks Sean. The place is really looking good. The Wheelers would have loved it."

"Do you love it?"

She nods and my ripped-up heart squeezes. "Good," I say, because making Summer happy is the most important thing in the world to me.

She opens her door and my phone pings. I pull it from my pocket and the text from Gram makes me smile. I hold the phone out. "Gram."

Summer's smile lights the cab. "I love that she texts."

"Come here." I reach for her, draw her mouth to mine and give her a kiss. "I'll see you at five." I watch her weave around the cars in the lot, and it's only after she's safely inside the pub, that I put the truck back into gear and head to the old homestead to see what Gram needs.

Warm air feels good against my face as I drive. I take the turn down the long road leading to the old house, and when I see Gram and Jamie on the front swing, the permanent knot in my stomach squeezes the air from my lungs. I climb from the truck and dust kicks up under my boots as I hurry toward them. I reach the top step and stop before the landing. My gaze goes from Gram, to Jamie back to Gram again.

"What's wrong?"

Gram tries to smile, and while she's tough, heck we all are because of her, this time she can't hide her pain. She's had so much loss, too.

"Funeral home called," she said, her voice a little softer than usual. Hands folded in her lap, I notice how tight they are, how hard this really is on her. "We need to go make arrangements."

"I thought we weren't having the service until everyone got home." Why is it there was some part of me that thought we'd never have to really face this, never have to put our father in the ground? He was always as hard as nails, a gale force wind that no one or nothing could stop. At least that's how he always seemed to me.

"Everyone is home," Jamie said, his eyes snapping up. "The last cousin got in last night." He gestures toward the door. "They're all inside, either eating or sleeping off the long trek home."

"Okay," I say, not really up to facing any of them right now. Fuck, I'd been so busy playing with Summer, I'd forgotten about my responsibilities, what I owe this family and the example I'm supposed to be setting. *Well fucking done, Sean.* I can just imagine what Dad would say about that. I swallow hard. "Gram, are you ready?"

Jamie stands. "I can take her."

"No," I say much too harshly, my boots echoing around the quiet homestead as I take the last step to the landing, to help Gram. I'm the oldest. It's what I need to do. Jamie nods and sits back down. I put my arm around Gram, and for the first time in my life I realize how small and fragile she really is. I swallow back the shit storm clawing at me, hollowing out my gut and pressing against my eyes.

I help Gram into the truck, and she gives me a feeble smile as I drive down the long lane leading to the main road. I don't need to ask to know where we're going. There is only one funeral home in town and the last time I was there I was a teenager. After mom's funeral, Jamie and I tore up the streets looking for a fight. But I'm older now, need to curb that shit and start acting like the adult I am.

"I met Jenna," Gram says, breaking the quiet and wanting to talk about something happier, I suppose.

I give her a quick look then turn my attention back to the road. "She's just a friend, Gram. You shouldn't have invited her to Sunday dinner."

"I invite everyone who's come to live in Blue Bay to dinner, you know that." She lifts her head. "Inviting her to dinner has nothing to do with you." I shake my head and grin. While she does invite every new resident to dinner, this still has everything to do with me.

"I know what you're up to," I say.

"Oh?"

"Yeah, you're hoping I'll find a wife and settle down here in Blue Bay. You don't have to worry. I'm home for good this time."

Green eyes gloss with worry and she fidgets with the big purse on her lap. "Sean, I don't want you to stay here if it's going to make you miserable. We have one shot at this life, and you need to find happiness. Your father would want you to be happy."

I could never make my father happy.

I eye her. "And you think Jenna is the happiness I'm looking for, the girl who's going to keep me in Blue Bay?"

Quick on her feet, she comes back with, "What part of 'inviting her to dinner has nothing to do with you' don't you understand?"

I laugh out loud as she bobs her head, always getting the one-up on me. "As long as it has nothing to do with me. And I know this is where I belong Gram. I can be happy here."

Her look is dubious, but instead of commenting she says,

"Jenna looks an awful lot like Summer Wheeler, don't you think? You always did have a thing for her."

Way to be subtle, and how she knew I always had a thing for Summer is beyond me. "She looks nothing like Summer," I say and jack the tunes. Gram grabs a Kleenex from her purse and wipes at her nose as we take the corner and turn on to Main Street.

My gaze slides over the streets, the tourists who are bustling about and all the shops open for business. My stomach clenches as my mind goes back. I used to know every inch of these streets, used to run them with my brothers. I knew when it was time to go home to dinner from the shadows on the sides of the buildings. I knew every crack in the cement, every car on the street. I can still smell the homemade ice cream and waffle cones at Sugar's, the apple pie at Benny's, the antiseptic in the corner drugstore. In the busy summers the briny scent of the ocean filled the air, the laughter of children playing in the water. When the leaves began to fall and the sultry summer turned to autumn, the air crisp and cooler, the tourists would pack up and leave—go back to their real lives for the winter months. The streets grew quiet then, the town once again belonging to the locals.

This town, with all its familiar shops and people is like a character of Blue Bay in and of itself. I feel a pinch in my chest, right around the vicinity of my heart. I missed this place, felt a little hollowed when I left it in my rearview mirror. Now that I'm back, everything is the same, yet different. Nothing is normal anymore. My dad is gone and Summer is back, living under an alias.

As my heart beats too fast, I abandon my trip down memory lane and squeeze my truck between two parked cars, then kill the ignition. The funeral home looms in front of us and for a minute I'm not sure I can do this. Dad was the pillar of the community. Him being gone just doesn't seem real. But when Gram reaches for the door, I press a fist to my eyes and pull myself together.

"Gram," I say, and touch her arm. "I can do this if you want to wait here."

Her smile is slow, and steady, like her. "You're a good boy, Sean. Let's do this together."

I jump from the truck and circle it to help Gram out. Clouds knit together overhead as the hot sultry air slides over my skin. Gram rubs her arthritic knuckles. "A storm is coming," she says.

I nod in agreement. But in my gut I know the storm building around me has nothing to do with the weather. No, this storm has been years in the making and has everything to do with the guilt swirling inside me, looking for an outlet. With an ominous feeling closing in on me, chasing me through the streets I once ruled, I lead Gram to the front doors, my legs like cement. The god-awful scent of cleanser and flowers falls over me as I usher Gram inside, and when nausea hits I try to breathe past it.

We're guided into a small room in the back, where we sit with the funeral director to go over the service, prayers, and reception. I take it all in, feel like I'm having a fucking out-of-body experience. Is this really happening? It all feels so surreal and I'm having a hard fucking time processing the information. By the time we leave and I drop Gram off back at the house I know I need one of two things: a hard bike ride or a hard fuck.

Probably both.

I jump on my Yamaha, tug on my helmet, and hit the throttle. I drive through town until I reach the next county. I meander along the coast and cruise the hills and valleys I know like the back of my hand. But something is missing. A ride always used to make me feel better, but today I need something more.

I turn around and head back to Blue Bay. Summer doesn't get off for another hour, but I can't wait that long. I ease into the lot of Winchesters and park beside Tyler's bike. I stomp to the front door, and when I push it open and see Summer with her hands on my fucking brother, my entire world compresses, fades to a dangerous shade of red as the sight before me knocks me off balance.

The door slams shut behind me, probably because I gave it a hard fucking shove, and all eyes turn to me. Tyler goes stiff, and Summer jumps back, the loud bang frightening her. Either that, or she hadn't expected to get caught running her fucking hands over Tyler's shoulder. I told her it was me and her this summer, no one else, and I fucking meant it.

She's not like that.

Everything in me screaming possession as I glare at Tyler and he jumps to his feet, meets my gaze straight on as I walk across the room to get up in his face.

"Back the fuck off," he says before I can get a word out. "Jenna was just helping me with my shoulder."

"What the fuck are you doing here?" I stand before him, practically nose to nose. "Don't you have a job to do?"

I take in his crossed arms, his hard expression. "No, I don't because you can't get the fucking permits," he shoots back. "What's your fucking problem, Sean?" he says through clenched teeth as he glowers at me.

I fist my hair, tug on it. *Shit. Shit. Shit.* This is my little brother and I'm two seconds from slamming my fist into his face because Summer had her hands on him. Ty would never disrespect me like that. None of the guys would. There isn't one Owens who'd hone in on his brother's girl. *Yeah, she's my fucking girl.* I'm just so fucked up inside after the trip to the funeral home, my heart so goddamn cut up, I'm not thinking straight.

I look at Summer, and in a deceptively calm voice say, "Get your things."

She's blinking rapidly, her gaze shifting around the room, but I don't care who is looking at us. In fact if any of the dickless assholes are here right now, I might make them my punching bag.

"My shift isn't over, Sean."

I take a deep breath, and let it out slowly in an effort to get my shit together. My boots scrape as I step up to her, my knuckles touching her. "Get your things," I say again, my voice calm, despite the motherfucking hurricane tearing through me.

As though she can see into my soul, see the fucked-up state I'm in, she nods. "I'll tell Beck I have to cut out early."

"I'll take care of Beck." I don't turn to Ty. Don't want to see his face. I feel like shit, but he's smart enough to know why, and if I see his sadness, his disappointment in me, I'm going to fucking lose it or punch something—neither of which I want.

I step in to Beck's office, take over his doorway. He lifts his head, and his face drops when he gets a glimpse of me. As he stares, I take a moment to consider what he sees. Every muscle in my body is tight, my hands are fisting, clenching and unclenching, and I probably have murder in my eyes. He doesn't speak. Instead, he pushes back in his chair and waits for me to say something.

"Jenna is cutting out early. It's on me, not her."

He nods. What else is he going to do? I'm in a mood and he's not going to stand in my way. I walk back into the pub and Summer is coming from the back room, her purse over her shoulder. Need slams in to me, beats at me like a drum. I fucking need her—for far too many reasons that frighten me.

"You okay on the back of my bike?" I ask.

She smiles, but it's forced. "As long as you avoid all hairpin turns."

Does she really think I'd do anything to hurt her? She attempts another smile to let me know she's kidding. But Jesus, I'm fed the fuck up with the lies. I'm Sean. She's Summer. I'd cut off my left nut if it meant protecting her. From the first time I set eyes on the skinny little freckle-faced blonde outside Sugar's, I was done for. So fucking done for.

I dip my head and my hair falls forward. "You know I'd never do anything to hurt you right?"

She goes quiet, those dark eyes moving over my face. "I know, Sean."

I capture her hand and silence falls over us as I lead her outside. Tyler's eyes drill into my back, but I don't turn. It's been a shit day, brutal as fuck helping Gram arrange for Dad's burial, and I need to escape for a few hours. We get outside, and I lead her to my bike. I unhook the spare helmet and place it on her head. She reaches for the clasp, but I push her hands away and do it for her. She gives a breathy huff, and I stare at her, daring her to say something. I told her when this affair began that I'd be doing things for her. She better not challenge me now. Not when I'm in this kind of mood.

I climb on the bike and she slides in behind me. "Hold on to me," I say and her hands slide around my waist as I pull into dinner-hour traffic. She doesn't ask where we're going, just holds me tight, her legs wrapped around my body squeezing hard. I'm not sure where I'm taking her, but after aimlessly driving for miles, I find myself on the bluff. When it comes right down to it, I guess I'm not surprised I drove here.

When we were kids we used to climb the bluff and dive headfirst into the water. Damn daredevils, every last Owens boy. The year Summer hit fourteen, God she was so pretty, her mother let her out of her sight more, and while her friends were allowed to go with us to the bluff, Summer was never allowed. Probably a good thing since she wasn't a strong swimmer.

Still, I remember my brothers making out with the girls, and I used to imagine bringing Summer here with me, kissing and swimming until day bled to night. But I never acted on my urges back then.

I climb from the bike and help her off. She makes a move to unclasp her helmet but I do it for her and hook them both on the handlebars. "Come on." Her hand slides into mine like it's the most natural thing in the world and for a second it gives me pause. I look at her, take in the concern in her eyes, and it guts me. Sweet Summer, she's worried about me but she's just as fucked up and lost as I am.

We climb the beaten-down grass path to the top of the bluff. With the rain coming, I don't expect anyone to be there. Only an idiot would be hanging at Blue Bay's highest ridge with a rainstorm brewing overhead. If Summer knew what was good for her, she'd run the other way, seek shelter. But she's not. She's sanding strong beside me, unafraid.

When we reach the top, I drop to the grass and cross my legs. Summer does the same and stays quiet beside me as we look out at the white caps crashing against the shore below us. Seconds turn to minutes, and we just breathe, our knees touching, her heat bringing warmth and light to my darkest corners.

"I told him I hated him and never want to see him again," I finally say, breaking the silence as every buried emotion I have comes roaring to the surface. Pain, pleasure, sorrow, and joy all hitting like a fucking lightning bolt. My body breaks out in a sweat and I angle my head to steal a glance at Summer, catch her reaction, but all she does is nod, and for that I'm grateful. To be honest, right now I don't want to be consoled or pitied or fucking lectured. I just need to get a lot of shit off my chest. Up until Summer there was no one I ever wanted to confide in, not even my brothers.

"He was a hard-assed son of a bitch. None of us guys could ever do anything right in his eyes. Every last one of us left him, left the family and business, never to look back." I swallow the bile punching into my throat, and take a couple fueling breaths. "I remember the day like it was yesterday. I was nineteen, and we were working on one of the cottages. Dad asked me to run to the hardware store to get some four-inch spikes. I was already huge into bikes at the time, and jumped on my Yamaha." I pause and laughed. "I loved that bike, saved every cent I ever made to get it." I pick at the grass beneath me. "Anyway, I got Dad's nails, but Benny flagged me down. He asked me to do a delivery. How could I say no to him right? He was like a hundred years old even back then."

Summer gives me a small smile. "That he was."

"So I did a quick delivery to help the guy out, and by the time I got the nails to Dad, he was fuming. He wouldn't let me explain the delay, and we both said some pretty nasty shit to each other that day. I threw the fucking nails at him, and walked out. I emptied my back account, stuffed some clothes into my backpack and took off. I wandered for a bit, did some odd jobs, then made some connections on the motocross circuit."

She nods like she knows this story. "You did well for yourself."

"How do you know that?"

"Oh, I . . . just assumed. When you put your mind to something you're the kind of guy who gives it his all."

"I never should have let my temper get the best of me. I was a stupid fucking kid, you know. I think back now, and I see Dad was just trying to make a man of me. Of all of us, really. Maybe he didn't know all the right things to say. Fuck knows he didn't know all the right thing to do." I scoff. "Maybe that's how his father treated him and it's the only way he knew to parent. It couldn't have been easy for him, trying to fill the shoes of both a mother and father." Edgy and out of sorts, I press my palm to my eyes, fight back the sting of tears and go quiet for a long time. "I went with Gram to make the funeral arrangements today. We bury him next Tuesday," I say quietly.

"I'll go with you." Her hand snakes out and closes over mine, and she just holds me, her look one of understanding, never judgment.

"I wish I would have come home sooner. I wish I could have apologized. We all turned our backs on him. I wish . . ." A sound catches in my throat. A half laugh, half cry. "I wish he knew I . . . loved him."

"He knew, Sean," she says quietly, no reprimand in her voice, just gentle understanding.

I bite down on my cheek. Fuck man, I don't want to cry. "I wish I could have made him proud of me, you know, but nothing I ever did was good enough. I nearly fucking killed myself on the circuit. I had something to prove. I just never knew if I was trying to prove something to him or me. Still, none of that shit is an excuse to tell him I hate him though. I didn't just walk out on him, I set an example for the rest of the guys in the family." I exhale slowly. "Stupid fucking kid."

"That's just it, Sean. You were just a kid. We all do stupid things as kids. That's our job, and our parents' job is to guide us into adulthood the best way they know how."

"If I ever have kids, which I never plan to, I'd never want to be such a hard ass."

"Dads are hard-asses and sometimes just plain stupid when it comes to raising kids. How can they just expect a child to step into their shoes and know the rules if they've never walked in them right?"

My heart skips a beat. She's talking about her own dad. Her voice is far too raw, too full of grief. Like she's dredging up painful memories. What kind of danger is she in?

She turns to me, her hair catching in the breeze. She pushes it back. "My dad always tried to protect me. I think they're very different with girls and boys."

I look out to see a sailboat bobbing in the distance. "Maybe it would have been different if there was a girl in the family. Might have softened him a bit."

"I can't believe you have a football team of boys and not one girl," she says, shaking her head.

"Gram is still holding out for great-grandkids."

"I always wanted a brother," she says. "You were lucky to grow up in a big family. I would have liked that, Sean. But Mom died, and Dad and I moved around a lot."

"I'm sorry."

"I never had a lot of friends because of it." She exhales slowly and looks around. "I don't feel so alone here."

"What happened to your dad?"

"He died in a motorcycle accident but . . ." Her voice falls off as she chokes back a cry.

I put my arm around her and she falls against me. "But what?"

She opens her mouth like she wants to say, then closes it again.

"Tell me about your mom."

She swallows, and that haunted look returns to her face. "I walked into her room one morning and found her dead on the bed. Brain tumor."

"Jesus," I say. I knew her mom had died and rumors went around but I never really knew the truth. "What a horrible thing to happen."

"Yeah, it was a long time ago."

But the pain was as raw today as it was back then. I can see it in her eyes.

"I talked to Gram about Sunday dinner. I tried to get you out of it."

"It's okay. I decided I would go."

"Yeah?" I pick a blade of grass and run it between my fingers.

"I've always wanted a big family. I used to think I'd have one of my own. The big house, white picket fence. Is that silly?"

"No it's not, and why did you say you 'used' to think you'd have one?" I ask.

She shrugs. "I just . . . ," she begins. Jesus, is she finally going to tell me what the fuck is going on in her life? "Don't think about that anymore," she says finishing the sentence.

"You should have that. You deserve that."

She turns from me, shadowing her face with her hair, but not before I see the moisture in her eyes. "Maybe while I'm here I can live vicariously through your family."

As I take in her smile and her acceptance of Gram's invitation, two things hit me: One, for the first time she's opening up to me, sharing a part of herself, and two, she's still talking about leaving, and I don't fucking want her to. What I do want is to ask her what the fuck is wrong and why she's been lying to me, but I'm too worried I might frighten her off. What if I come straight out and ask her and it scares her away. She's running, I get that, but how the fuck can I watch over her, and protect her if she runs away from me?

"You say that now. Wait until you're surrounded by us, nowhere to run. You'll be wondering what you ever got yourself in to."

"I'm not worried. You'll be with me, and there isn't one Owens boy who will stand up against you."

I pinch the bridge of my nose, and curse myself. "Tyler was ready to."

"He understands, Sean. He's knows how hard today was on you. You were pushing. He was pushing back. He's hurting, too, you know."

My chest grows tight, like I've been kicked in the ribs. "Yeah, I know."

She gives me a small smile and I fall back onto the grass, dragging her down with me. "I think we all just wish we could have made him proud of us one way or another."

"Is that why you've taken over the business? To prove to him you can be the man he needs you to be? Make him proud of you once and for all?"

"Yeah. I sunk my entire savings into the business and if I can't get the fucking permits I need, it will all be for nothing."

I turn my head and gaze at her as she stares at the dark clouds bursting with moisture. The rain will be here any minute. With unhurried movements, like we have all the time in the world and she doesn't care if the skies open up and douse us in water, her hand slides across the grass.

"It means protection," I say.

"What?"

"My tattoo," I begin. "When we were in the bathroom last week, you asked what it meant."

"I remember."

"The scorpion. It represents protection. I chose it because I'd do anything for my brothers and cousins." I swallow against the tightness in my throat. "And my father," I add quietly. "But I did a piss-poor job of that, didn't I?"

"You're a good man, Sean. The best man I know," she whispers, her voice soft, whispering over me like the ocean breeze, and creating an intimacy deeper than anything I've ever felt before.

When she reaches for me, links her fingers it mine, her soft touch is like a healing balm to my soul, able to ease the pain inside of me—calm my demons. In that instance my body aches for hers, needing her in a way I've never needed another.

"You're not going to tell me I'm sweet again are you?" I say, needing like fuck to lighten things up. The truth is I've never opened myself up to emotions. Didn't want to let anyone in, only to end up disappointing them. But with Summer, all that has changed.

She grins and turns toward me, going up on one elbow as she fixes her attention on me. "Maybe," she says, her warm breath brushing my skin, turning me inside out. Need resonates through me. I don't know how I thought I could ever fuck her out of my system. This is Summer Wheeler we're talking about. Not some circuit girl accustomed to my one-night stands. I take in the freckles on her nose and baser instincts kick in. I need her beneath me, need to be inside her, need to strip her naked so I can put my mouth all over her.

"Then maybe I owe you that spanking, after all."

She rolls from me, offering me her ass, her body. "Maybe you do."

Yeah, sure I asked for sex and she's given me her body numerous times, but maybe I fucking want more. Jesus, I've never wanted a woman like this before. My bedroom always had a revolving door, and I rarely slept with the same woman twice. No ties. No commitments. Just fun. That's the motto I lived by. So why the fuck is this woman messing with that?

I take a quick moment to reevaluate our relationship, and suddenly I want to ask for things I never thought I'd ever ask for. Summer has always been everything to me. Like a goddamn burst of sunshine on a gray winter's day. Unlike most people, she never judged, and saw things in me no one else did and it's time I stop denying what I really want from her—to have her in my life, as well as my bed. No fucking way can I walk away from this thing between us.

In the blink of an eye life can change. We're both aware of that. Maybe Gram was right. We have one shot at this and need to find happiness. Maybe I would be happy staying here in Blue Bay if Summer was staying here with me. When I first came back, I figured I had to walk the straight and narrow—no distraction, no women, no trouble. I thought that was what I would take to be the man Dad needed me to be, but I see now that Summer makes me a better man. She believes in me, knows I'll never hurt her, and that helps me believe in myself, believe that I'm not a guy who only knows how to disappoint. I mull that over, let the idea of it grow on me. But Summer still has secrets, is still hiding things from me.

I tune everything out, even the light raindrops falling on us, and gaze at the woman I've been crazy about since we were kids. Something that feels like love moves through me and I know I have a long-ass way to go to get my father's business up and running the way he'd want me to, but that road doesn't seem so steep or painful if Summer is by my side. But what does she want? Is it possible that I could prove she can trust me, prove that we could move past the secrets and build something together?

What if that's not what she wants?

What if it is?

12

SUMMER

I can't believe I'm sitting around a huge dining room table with Sean and all his family. The noise level has reached an all-time high as his twin brothers razz Tyler about some girl he's been hanging out with. Tyler jumps from the table, and takes them both to the floor in record time but stops instantly when Grandma Nellie puts her hand on her hips and glares at them.

For such a small woman, she sure has her grandsons under control. I take in her scowl, one I've become familiar with in her grandsons, and realize she's the glue that holds this whole family together. She turns to Tyler and points her spatula.

"Who is this girl that has you all tied up in knots?"

Sulking, Ty sits down, and even though I can tell he's trying hard to shut down his expression, there is a light in his eyes as Grandma Nellie talks about the mysterious girl who has, undoubtedly, gotten under his tattooed skin. "No one, Gram."

She shakes her head. "Don't tell me, then. I'll find out on Facebook later."

I smile, loving the camaraderie of this family, the way they fight and tease but so openly love each other. There isn't a man in here who wouldn't fight to the death to protect his brother. This is the family I always wanted. I ease back in my chair to take it all in, bask in the ambience of love and solidarity known as the Owens brothers.

"Gram . . . she's just a friend," Ty groans. But her scowl stops him.

I turn my head to hide a laugh, having no doubt that by this time next week—like Sean—Tyler will be sitting with his girl at his side.

His girl.

I steal a glance at the handsome man beside me, take in the scruff on his chin, his hard jawline that always softens when he looks at me. I might be his girl—but it's just for the summer season, or until he finishes work on the cottage, which, at the rate he's going, will be sooner rather than later. Eventually I'll have to get back to my life in SoCal. My heart grows heavy at that thought. Cripes, what the heck is that all about? SoCal is where I built my practice, have my home. I just need to find the ledger, and figure out what to do with it. I just pray it has answers to what really happened between my dad and Jack. But if I find what I'm looking for, who do I trust with the information?

Chatter around the table turns to the business, and all faces sober as they discuss the permits that Sean still isn't able to secure, and how they're going to lose the bid on the Cassidy cottage if he doesn't produce them soon. I consider my chiropractor business and the permits Sean needs, and my mind goes to one client in particular: Susie Jennings. I don't have many friends, but we hit it off and had coffee a few times outside of work. She's a nurse and I remember her mentioning she had a sister who worked for city hall back home I wonder if I could put a call in to her, ask her what Sean needs to do, how he can work around the red tape to finally secure the documents he needs. If I call, will my ex be able to track me? If I don't, what will happen to Sean's business? He so desperately wants it to work, to prove to his father once and for all he's the man he needed him to be. I have to do something. He's been so good to me, so caring and helpful and always there when I need him.

Grandma Nellie, along with the help of Jace, one of Sean's cousins—apparently he used to be a chef in New York—finish putting the dishes on the table. The delicious smell of pot roast fills the air and takes me back in time. My mom used to make the best pot roast. My heart fills with loss, but when Sean reaches under the table and gives my leg a squeeze, like he knows what's going on inside my head, the pain of loss isn't quite as hurtful as it used to be.

It's a shame this guy doesn't want a family or kids. He'd be such an amazing father, so aware of his shortcomings in parenting that he'd do his best to give his child everything they needed. When it comes to being a husband, he checks all the boxes, and I can't imagine a woman would want anyone else.

I don't want anything more.

Well done, Summer. Well done. This is a brief affair, and you'd be wise to remember that.

Grandma Nellie turns her attention my way, and far too many sets of eyes zero in me, but it's easy to tell they're happy the attention isn't on them. "It sure is nice having a female around the house," she says, as she scoops mashed potatoes out of a bowl and passes it on.

"It's nice to be here," I say, and mean it. I really do like being around these boys. I can see why my mother kept me away all those years ago. The Owens boys are a motley crew with bad reputations, but when it comes right down to it, under the tattoos and hard layers built over time, they're all nice guys.

Grandma Nellie winks at me. "I'm hoping one of these days I get myself a great-granddaughter to spoil."

"Gram," all the guys groan in unison.

"Mind your manners," she says, and they all shut up. "I was talking to Jenna here."

Sean looks at me and mouths the words, "Sorry."

I just grin. "A great-granddaughter is a wonderful thing to look forward to."

"You'd think one of these boys would have made that happen by now." Again they guys all groan and roll their eyes.

"You would think," I say and all glares are directed my way.

In a show of protectiveness, Sean puts his arm around me, and even though he's shielding me from his brothers and cousins, he says, "Not you, too."

Grandma Nellie smiles at me and my heart squeezes. My grandparents on either side died before I knew them, but I picture them all tough, yet tender, like the strong woman before me. "Us girls have to stick together."

"We do," I agree.

"Then you'll join me for antiquing tomorrow," she says, a statement not a question.

Sean laughs and I shake my head at him. How is it that Grandma Nellie has a knack for getting what she wants, much like the man beside me? I laugh and say, "Sure. I would love to go antiquing with you tomorrow."

Grandma Nellie has a grin on her face as she digs into her pot roast, and around the table the guys do the same. I watch for a moment, a feeling of warm contentment inside my belly.

Once the meal is done and dishes cleared, Sean says, "We need to go, Gram. Jenna needs to take Scout for a walk."

"Scout?"

"Her new pup."

"Fine. But I'll see you tomorrow, Jenna," she says and I give her a hug.

"I'll pick you up first thing in the morning," I say. Tomorrow is my day off, and I didn't have any other plans other than trying figure out what the key belonged to. I know it should be my number-one priority, and it is, but sometimes it's so easy to get caught up in this laid-back life here in Blue Bay.

We step outside and Sean comes around my side to open the truck door for me. "Sweet, and a gentleman," I say.

"Gram's watching, and if I didn't open the door for you, she'd gristle me."

"Gristle?" I tease.

"Believe me, you don't want to know." He grins, and adds, "And stop saying I'm sweet."

He circles the truck and I can't seem to wipe the smile off my face. I really enjoyed getting to know his family better, even though it's probably not in my best interest. I leave here soon and I'm not supposed to get too close.

"What are you grinning about?" Sean asks as he climbs in beside me.

I let my gaze move over his hard body, and a slow tremor moves through me. "Your family."

"I warned you."

I give him a little punch. "I loved them, Sean."

He turns to me, and a smile touches him mouth. "Yeah?"

"Yeah."

"They loved you, too. Except for when you sided with Gram," he teases.

We both go quiet like we suddenly realize we're tossing the "L" word around. I stare out the window as we drive through town and when we reach the cottage, and jump from the truck we can hear Scout barking at the noise from inside.

"She's going to make a great watchdog," I say.

Sean unlocks the front door, and my heart wobbles when he opens Scout's kennel and she jumps all over him. He drops to his knees and plays with her. Sean is big and tough, yes so soft and gentle with the little pup. It's the sweetest thing I've ever seen and if I wasn't in love with him before this I sure would be now.

Jesus, I'm in love with Sean.

"You ready for your walk, girl?" he asks, and Scout's tail is wagging so hard, she's knocking herself off balance. As I work to catch my breath at that revelation, one I always knew but had never admitted to myself until now, I push past them and grab Scout's leash.

"Want to head into town?" I ask, keeping my voice light to disguise the barrage of emotions taking up residency in my heart. "Grab an ice cream?"

Sean nods and hooks the leash to Scout, and we start up the big hill leading to the center of town. I look up at him, take in his handsome profile.

"Sean."

"Yeah?"

"What the heck is antiquing?"

He laughs. "It's you and Gram hitting every antique shop from here to three counties over and back again. Have fun with that."

I whack him. "Be nice."

"No way. You sided with Gram about great-grandchildren, and got what you deserve. Don't for a minute think I'm even going to try to get you out of it."

I lift my head. "Fine, I was going to bring you a Starbucks back from Hope Falls, but now you can forget it. I'll think about you as I enjoy my Americano, though."

Her arches a brow and shoots back with, "Are you forgetting that I like the local coffee?"

I crinkle my nose, and swipe my tongue over my bottom lip. "Sometimes, there's just no accounting for taste."

His grin is sensually wicked. "You keep talking like that, and I'm going to find you something else to do with that smart mouth of yours," he says, and I shiver at his low, rough words.

"Promises, promises," I tease, and take off running.

Sean and Scout catch up with me when I reach Sugar's, but I'm the only one out of breath. Sean ties Scout to the lamppost outside the ice cream shop.

I frown, and glance up and down the busy street. "Do you think she'll be okay out here?"

"We're in Blue Bay, Jenna. We don't even lock our doors around here."

"Right." Sometimes I forget that I'm a long way from home, and Blue Bay is like a completely different universe. Still, that doesn't mean I should let my guard down, the way I've been doing lately. I take that moment to look over my shoulder.

Sean opens the door and ushers me inside. The delicious scent of waffle cone hits as we enter the store. I order a chunky monkey and Sean gets chocolate, and a small doggy bowl full of vanilla for Scout. Scout is yipping as we come out, obviously excited for her first ice cream. Sean feeds her a bit and she starts to hop around.

I laugh. "Great, now she's hyped up on sugar," I say. "We'll never get any sleep tonight."

Sean eyes me, his gaze dropping to my tongue as I lick my cone. The muscles along his jaw tighten, and heat flashes in the depths of his gaze. "I don't think sleep is on the agenda anyway." A quiver moves through me, and I grab his hand.

"Come on, let's walk."

We enjoy our cones as we head toward the bus station, the

key in my back pocket practically burning a hole in my jeans. I've yet to see if it opens a locker at the station—the only place I haven't tried yet—but I'm not sure that's wise at the moment. I touch my back pocket, feel the outline of the key. Sean sees an old friend across the street, and waves, but the friend has other ideas. He darts between cars and stops us.

"Hey, Graham," Sean says. "Long time. This is Jenna."

I exchange pleasantries with Graham, who reminds me of an insurance salesman. Sean is about to push past him, but Graham decides he wants to talk about old times with Sean, even though I can't image they shared a history. It does, however allow me to disappear for a second. I quickly excuse myself, letting Sean know I'm going to dart into the bus station to use the washroom.

He looks mortified that I'm leaving him alone with Graham, but he's a big boy and can handle himself. Not wanting to lie, I dart to the washroom and when I come out I step up to the rows of lockers. I pull the key from my back pocket. I wish it had a number on it. That would probably make the search that much easier.

I try a few different locks, and when it gets stuck in one, my heart races. The last thing I want to do is break if off in one of the locks. It holds the secret to my father's death. I'm certain of it.

"Everything okay?" Sean asks, his voice right there at my back. Jeez, I hadn't even heard him approach.

I turn and his brows are pulled together, perplexed. "Yeah, I just got my key stuck."

"Here." His big hand closes over the key and after a few jiggles, he frees it. He looks over the key, examines it carefully. His face is sober, harsh, his eyes deadly as they meet mine. "What's with this key, anyway?"

I shrug and make light. "Nothing really. Just found it and I'm curious about it, I guess."

He stares at me for a long time, his body hard, lethal, like he's itching for a fight. I try not to fidget. I really hate lying to him, but under the circumstances I have no choice.

"Jenna—"

"We should probably get back. Poor Scout looks exhausted."

Sean glances down at the pup, who is laid out at his feet. He scoops her up and we walk back to the house. Both of us a little quieter. When we get inside and my heart swells with the things I feel for Sean as he settles Scout into her bed. Needing a moment, I make my way to the bathroom for a shower.

I turn the water on, and when footsteps herald Sean's approach, I spin. His gaze drops to my mouth and moving with purpose he tugs off his shirt. He steps up to me, touches me with intimate recognition. Warmth floods my system and my breath quickens. I touch him, my hands roaming, unable to get enough. I know I'm in too deep with him, and despite every alarm bell ringing in warning, I can't help but want him. I step into the shower, crook my finger, and whisper, "What was that you said about finding another use for my smart mouth?"

13

SUMMER

"What do you think of this piece?" Gram asks. She lowers herself into an old rocking chair, and runs her weathered fingers over the shiny wood, a small smile on her face like the piece takes her back in time.

"I think it's beautiful. You should get it."

"I had a chair just like this. Used to rock the grandbabies to sleep." She chuckles and pushes back and forth as if she's cradling them now. "But after my own boys, and eight grand-kids, the old thing fell apart."

"Gram," I say—she insisted I call her that. "What was Sean's dad like?" I ask since she opened the door for discussion.

She smiles, and looks past my shoulders like she's deep in thought. "He was a good boy growing up, and turned into a fine man. He loved all his boys, despite their antics." She rolls her eyes, and gives a little laugh. "Those kids," she begins. "Well let's just say they old saying, 'boys will be boys' definitely applies to them."

I laugh. "Poster boys for authority issues," I add and when

she turns those intelligent green eyes on me I realize my slip. "I mean . . . that's what Summer told me."

She nods. "Sean always did have a thing for that girl."

"He did?" My pulse leaps. "How do you know that?" I ask, my words a little too quick, giving away a little too much.

"A grandmother knows these things, child." She exhales slowly, and the action reminds me of Sean. "But back to Sean's dad: he was particularly hard on Sean."

"Because he was the oldest?"

She nods, her green eyes a bit glossy. "He wanted him to set an example for the others. Said he was too soft, like his mother, and wanted to toughen him up." Sadness moves over her face. "All it did was drive Sean away. I didn't always agree with Carl's methods, but he meant well and had one thing right. There isn't an Owens boy who doesn't take after their mother and she was a good woman."

"Sean is a good man."

"The best."

I'm not sure how much I should be saying, but the overwhelming urge to better understand Sean and his father's relationship tugs at me. The floorboards creak as I take a step, and run my hand over an antique dresser, I catch my reflection in the mirror, and fix my hair. Gram meets my gaze and I say, "I think Sean holds lot of guilt."

She wags her fingers. "The boy has nothing to be guilty about."

I turn back to her and lean against the dresser. "I think he wished he could have made his dad proud of him."

Gram's head rears back, and she steeples her fingers in front of her chest. "There isn't a father in this whole state more proud of his son than Carl was of Sean. He was proud of all his boys."

"Really?" My heart fills with warmth, so happy to hear that.

She looks down, emotions playing on her face. "When we get home I need to show you something."

I nod, curious about what it is she wants to show me, as Gram pushes herself out of the rocking chair and turns her attention to some old china plates. She shuffles around a bit, taking it all in, then asks to go to the next antique shop, in the next town. We hit a few more stores, and after a long day, I pull into Gram's driveway. She invites me in for tea, and I agree because I'm anxious to see what it is she wants to show me.

Now here it is, hours later and I'm feeling a little off, a little emotional as I walk around the quiet cottage and draw all the curtains. I haven't seen much of Sean today, and tonight—the night before the funeral—I insisted he stay with his family. But now the place seems so empty, a little bit eerie without him. Sure I have Scout, but she's still a pup, and while her bark might sound scary, the sweet little lab wouldn't hurt a fly.

As I stifle a yawn, I walk through the cottage and head to the kitchen to fill the kettle with water. After antiquing all day, and grabbing a few inexpensive art pieces for the cottage, I'm rather tired. But before I go to bed and face a hard day with Sean tomorrow, there is a call I have to make.

I drop down onto the sofa, and Scout jumps up and curls in to me. I rub her fur, and grab my cell phone, to check my contacts, glad I hadn't tossed it now. When I come across Sue Jennings number, I reach for the landline. I registered the phone under Jenna Garridy, not Summer Wheeler, so I'm praying to God my ex can't track it. I have no doubt he's keeping a close eye on my cell, even though I've not used it since I fled home a few weeks ago.

I punch in her number, it rings four times, and just as I'm about to hang up, Sue comes on. Before I left, I had my secretary cancel all my appointments indefinitely, and I fully expect Sue to be curious about that.

She answers, and is surprised to hear me on the other line.

"Is everything okay?" she asks cautiously.

"Everything is fine," I say, and inject a lightness into my voice.

"Caller display says your calling from a 203 area code. Where are you?"

Shit. Shit. Shit. When I arranged for the phone, I asked for "private" to display, not my damn number. I make a mental note to call the phone company in the morning.

"Just a family thing I had to take care of." Over our coffee chats, I didn't delve too deeply in to my personal life. She knows I'd been dating Jack, but has no idea that outside of the Owenses I have no family. Wait, what? The Owenses aren't my family. I'm just living vicariously through Sean while here in Blue Bay. "I wanted to ask you a question."

"Sure," she says.

I spend the next few minutes asking her how to get around the red tape at city hall, and how a friend's business is getting held up on permits.

"Let me call my sister and I'll get back to you."

I freeze for a second. Is her calling me back a good idea? What if Jack has her phone tapped, or is listening in to the conversation. Then again, I'd never mentioned Susie to Jack so he has no idea were friends. Unless, of course, he'd been watching me.

"How about I call you back in a half an hour," I say.

A moment of silence and then, "Are you sure everything is okay?"

"Perfectly fine, just wanting to help a friend out."

She hesitates, then says, "Okay, half hour."

I hang up and pace, and pray to freaking God, I'm not making a mistake. I count down the minutes and when I finally call her back, the only suggestions her sister was able to give was to find a way to get the officer off my friend's back, or pay off town hall, because maybe that's the way things are done in small towns. Since I have no idea how to convince Walker to back down, and have no money to pay off town hall, I hang up, no further ahead than when I started. Feeling a little lost, I make my tea, and head to the bedroom to watch reruns of *Gilmore Girls* on my old laptop.

I fall asleep during the show, and a loud bang wakes me up before dawn. Beside me on the bed, Scout growls. With my heart running a marathon, I pull her to me, and tuck her under the blankets, praying to God it's nothing but another raccoon. Sean would want me to call him, but he had enough to deal with yesterday, and today, well, burying his father is going to be hell on him—on them all. I steal a glance at the bag in the corner, the proof that Sean's dad was proud of him. I'll have to tell him eventually, show him the evidence, but when, how? He's going through so much already.

Sleep doesn't come easily after the crash outside my cottage, and after a restless night, I grope my way to the coffeemaker. This morning I don't much care if the coffee tastes like dishwater, I'm desperate for a cup or two. I open the front door, let Scout out on the lawn to do her morning business, and breathe in the fresh air. I leave the door open behind me, and step outside to glance up and down the quiet street, so peaceful this time of day. I walk around the corner and find my trash bins tipped over again, and feel a measure of relief that it was just another raccoon. After sniffing around for a good fifteen minutes, Scout finally comes running back to me.

I fill her bowls with food and water, and grin when I see her tail wagging so hard she's ready to fall over.

"Let me have a quick shower and I'll take you out for a longer walk."

I hurry to the shower, and the coffeepot is full and waiting by the time I finish. With nothing but a towel around my body, I pour a cup, but a strange sensation moves over me. I spin around, the hot java spilling over the side of my cup. *Shit.* I set it on the counter and wipe my hand as my gaze dart to every corner, only to find them empty—no boogeyman, no ex ready to "apply pressure to get the ledger once and for all." Still, the tingling doesn't stop, so I inch open the back curtain and peer out. It's still early, and other than a few sun worshipers lying flat out on the sand, no one is around. Must just be my imagination getting the better of me.

I try to shake off the uneasy feeling and throw on a pair of shorts and T-shirt. "Come on, girl," I say to Scout. I leash her and we head to the water for a nice long walk along the beach. Sand squishes between my toes and Scout barks and nips at the waves. She's such a silly girl. I'm already crazy about her. How I'll ever leave her when I go back home is beyond me. I'd love to take her but my place in the city has no room for a big dog.

After a long walk, we go back home. I don't care what Sean says about locking the doors. I've kept mine locked since I arrived. Well, except for the first day when Sean let himself in. But today, having the sense that someone is watching me, I lock them and double-check them. It's nearing noon by the time I head to my bedroom to pick out something appropriate for the funeral. I tug on a black blouse, black dress pants, and my low-heeled shoes.

The funeral starts at one, but I decide to go to the church early, in case the family needs me for anything. I tuck Scout into her bed, and jump into Dad's truck. The traffic is a lot busier now, and I realize it's because every vehicle in town is headed to the church Sean's dad must have been very well liked in this community—with the exception of Officer Walker, of course.

I park and slip from the truck, recognizing so many familiar faces as I make my way inside the church. I keep my head down, hair forward, hoping no one recognizes me in return. Once inside I see Sean and his family in the main foyer, greeting all those who've come to pay respect. Sean's eyes are downcast, his expression pained. I've never seen him so intense, yet so wide open and vulnerable.

As if sensing me, his head lifts when I enter, and our gazes collide. He attempts a smile but I can tell it's forced. My heart clenches. I want nothing more than to go to him, hug him, and tell him everything will be okay. I follow the long line and make my way to Sean. All the boys are dressed in suits and ties, looking so put together and handsome, I can hardly believe it's the same motley crew who own the back table at Winchesters. Sean pulls me to him, holds me far too long, and when he lets go, he keeps his hands on my shoulder.

He puts him mouth next to my ear, his warm breath washing over me, as he whispers, "Thanks for coming."

"Of course," I say.

He straightens to his full height and his eyes go narrow as they move over my face. "Are you okay?"

I nod. Isn't that just like Sean? He's going through hell and is worried about me. Warmth and admiration seep into my soul. "It's a sad day," I say, not about to tell him I've been spooked since I got out of bed this morning. "I'll go get a seat."

"Take the second row. It's reserved for family."

"Sean I'm not—"

"Take the second row, child," Gram says, and I just nod.

I slide into the second row, and organ music plays as the church fills up. There are so many people they had to bring in extra chairs, and even the lobby is full of those who couldn't fit inside. Sean and his family take their seats, and Sean sits in front of me. I put my hand on his shoulder, give a little squeeze, then sit back in my seat for the service.

By the time the minister finishes there isn't a dry eye in the house. I never really knew Sean's dad, but after listening to stories, I feel like I've known him my whole life.

We all leave the church to head to the cemetery, and Sean catches up to me in the parking lot. "Drive with me," he says, sounding a bit breathless, like he's been running.

I take one look at him, see the haunted look in his eyes and nod. We climb into his truck. "What about Gram?"

"She's traveling with the minister and Dad's ashes."

I nod and Sean slides his hand across the seat. He holds on to my hand so tightly, I'm sure he's going to break my fingers, but I don't say a word. His movements are slow, almost robotic when we slide from the truck and make our way to the burial site where his mom had been buried many years before.

"They're going to be together again," I say to Sean, wanting him to see something bright in this day.

"Yeah," is all he says in return as he hauls me into the shelter of his big body. He holds me like that during the burial process, then everyone heads back to Gram's homestead for the reception and to honor Carl's life.

The house is alive and noisy when we get there, everyone snacking and sharing memories of Carl. Sean greets everyone, speaks to his brothers, cousins and Gram, then comes to find me.

"Let's go."

"Sean—"

"I need air," he says.

Understanding his need to escape, we step outside and I climb on the back of his bike. We drive aimlessly and then end up back at my cottage. Sean uses his key to let us in, then plunks himself down on my sofa. He stares out the window, like he's escaped into himself, waging some internal war. My throat tightens to the point of pain. I've never seen him so lost and broken before.

"I'll make coffee," I say. I hurry to the kitchen as Scout jumps on Sean's lap. I hear him playing with her, and when I come back with the coffee, he's running his hand along the bulging wall.

"All that's left is to fix this wall," he says, his voice so distant I wonder what's really going through his mind.

"Sean," I say. He spins and I take in the tightness in his jaw and he looks past me, like he's not really seeing me at all. "Are you okay?"

A strange sound crawls out of his throat and he fists his hands and presses them to his eyes, but not before I see the torment on his face. "No, I'm not fucking okay."

"I'm sorry," I say, and set the cups down. I step into his arms and he grips my hair as he drags me into a tight embrace. Today was so hard on him. The guilt he's feeling is eating him up. I think about that, and while I'm not sure now is the right time, I don't know when it ever will be.

"I need to show you something," I say, my tears staining his suit jacket. I inch back and wipe my nose. "Why don't you get out of your suit? Get comfortable. You have some clothes here. I'll get them for you."

He tears at his tie as I turn and hurry to my room. I take a huge breath, praying to God I'm doing the right thing as I grab the bag Gram gave me. I reach into the laundry basket and pull out a pair of jeans and T-shirt that he'd left here.

I step back into the room and find him in nothing but his nicely fitting boxers. I hand him the clothes but he doesn't bother putting them on. Instead he drops into the sofa, sinking into the cushions.

"Sean," I begin and drop to the floor in front of him. He opens his legs and I shimmy in close, my hands on his thighs, the position so natural for us. "Your father was very proud of you. You left because he was hard on you, and in some ways he drove you away. He was just being a dad, and you were just being his son. None of that means you guys didn't love each other."

He shakes his head. "Don't—"

"Please, just hear me out."

Lacking his calm steadiness, he exhales, and runs a shaky hand through is hair. "Okay," he says, his voice sounding worn and tired as he regards me warily.

I reach into the bag, and pull out a DVD. I pop it from the plastic case and slide it into the DVD player. Sean remains silent as he watches, but his brow furrows like he has no idea what's going on. And why would he know? None of this was ever shared with him before.

The sound of his souped-up two stroke roars through the quiet room, and Sean leans forward, braces his elbows on his knees as he stares at the TV.

"What is this?" he asks when he sees himself on the screen, one of his old races playing out on the television. He shakes his head. "I don't understand. Where did you get this?"

I take the bag and empty it on the floor, showcasing the dozens of DVDs. "From Gram."

"How did Gram get these?"

"From your father."

He sits there, perplexed for a moment, then when understanding dawns, he sinks back into the sofa and covers his face with his hands. His chest rises and falls rapidly as he breaths through the shock. The sight of him sitting there so still, brings tears to my eyes.

I step back up to him, settle myself on the floor between his legs. "He was so proud of you, Sean. Gram told me he taped and watched and rewatched all your races. Some of these DVDs look like they've been played hundreds of times."

A muffled noise comes from behind his hands. Body tight, eyes watery, he says, "I . . . I didn't know."

My throat clogs and my insides turn to mush. "You said your one regret was never making him proud. He was always proud of you, Sean. Even when you were working construction with him and felt you couldn't do anything right in his eyes. He might have been a hard-ass, but is that such a bad things. Look at the man you are today."

"I'm not—"

"You're not an asshole, a jerk, a man who cares only about himself. You've always been there for me. Right from that first night you saved me from the drunk guy at Dick's Driving Inn and Diner to the night you stayed with me here at the cottage when I was spooked." For as long as I can remember, Sean was there for me—all lean muscle, strong and protective, ready to rescue me. "You're there for your gram, your brothers, your community. You're the best man I know, Sean."

His fists fall from his face, and I take in the red in his eyes. One hand slides around my head and he pulls me to him, for a deep, yet tender kiss. His tongue slides into my mouth, tangles gently, softly, and then he stands, scoops me up and carries me to the bedroom. I rest my head against his chest, my emotions on a roller-coaster ride as I feel his strong heartbeat.

I am so lost in this man.

He might be intense and troubled but I trust him. Maybe I should tell him what's going on in my life. He deserves that much from me. But what if I drag him and his family in to my troubles and one of them got hurt? I could never live with myself if that happened.

He dips his head. "I need to be inside you," he says quietly, a new calmness about him, a tenderness I've never seen before. I can almost feel the last shards of ice and coldness inside him thaw. "Tell me you need that, too." His voice wavers, softens, and a surge of love rushes to my heart.

"I need that, too," I say. I meet his glance, his eyes are so full of want and need, it generates a warmth and desire inside me. His mouth takes possession of mine and I palm his hard muscles, taking pleasure in his sculpted biceps and shoulders.

With need buzzing through my body, he sets me on my feet and I press my mouth to his bare chest. His body softens, relaxes as I breathe in the familiar scent of his skin. I kiss a path downward, my mouth trailing all over his flesh until I'm on my knees before him. A quick tug, and I have his boxers around his thighs, his hard cock jutting out at me. I acknowledge the flare of desire in me as I take him into my mouth. His sounds of pleasure curl around me, filling my heart with love. Need whispers through my blood as I pleasure him, and I want to give him more . . . everything . . . every last part of me.

He rocks his hips into me, his hands in my hair controlling the motions. I cup his balls, massage lightly, and he growls. I'll never tire of those sounds he makes when he's lost in pleasure. His veins fill with blood and I track one with my tongue.

"Come here," he whispers. I stand, and his fingers close over mine, warm and strong. His face softens and his body relaxes as we just hold each other. "I want you so much," he murmurs into my hair.

"Then take me," I say. His big fingers go to the buttons on my blouse. He takes his time to pop them. My glance moves over his handsome features, as he pushes the material from my shoulders. He sucks in a breath as I stand before him in my pants and bra. His eyes are filled with such tenderness, heat and need explode inside me.

"You are so beautiful," he whispers, and slides a strong

arm around me to unhook my lace bra. It too falls to the floor and he dips his head to take a nipple into his mouth. My body spasms with pleasure as his lips close around one hard nub. He licks and sucks and drag his tongue over my flesh, swirling back and forth until I'm whimpering in bliss. I cry out, and reach for him when he breaks the connection.

"I need to taste all of you." I nod as he kisses a path downward and sinks to his knees. The warmth of his breath elicits a shiver from deep within me. He goes back on his heels, and I brush my fingers over his face. He leans into my hand, and my entire world turns inside out. We've had sex, been together intimately numerous times, but I've never felt a connection to this man like I'm feeling right now. He reaches up, touches my mouth, then brushes his fingers over my neck, between my breasts, and my stomach, stopping when he reaches the button on my pants.

"I need you," he murmurs, the soft warmth of his voice covering me like a protective blanket as the hiss of my zipper sends little shivers along my spine. "I need you so fucking much."

"Please," I say, opening myself to him completely. He slides my pants to my ankles, and the key that has been pretty much permanently attached to me since I opened the lockbox Dad gave me, falls out of my back pocket and clangs on the wood floor. Sean looks at it for a moment, but says nothing as he picks it up and places it on the nightstand.

I kick off my pants, and with exquisite gentleness, he removes my panties, his caresses are slower, softer than ever before, the drag of his fingers touching me in places so deep, I know I'll never be the same again.

Once I'm naked he stands, removes his shorts, and presses his mouth to mine. He kisses me with such passion it leaves me gulping for my next breath. His hands span my waist. Honest to God, I've never felt such an easy intimacy with anyone before. Heat pours from his body to mine and back again as we hold one another like our lives depend on it. Strong arms circle my body and he pulls me to him, cocooning me in a bubble of safety and warmth.

With emotions ruling, I step back and fall onto the bed. I crook my finger, inviting him to join me. He growls and stands there for a moment longer, his gaze roaming my naked body. My breath catches. God, the needy way he looks at me nearly stops my heart.

He crawls over me, pins me with his weight as he takes my hands and holds them over my head, like he wants me at his mercy. He presses openmouthed kisses to my body, and slides between my legs. He pushes a finger into me as he laps at my clit. I rock into him and whimper, desperate for him to fill me.

"Please, Sean . . ."

He grips my hips, falls on top of me and slides into me, making me feel so gloriously full, I cry out in ecstasy. He pushes deeper, taking his time. Slow and steady, that's my Sean. My hands skim his sinewy muscles, explore his body, unable to touch enough, get him close enough. I wrap my legs around him as he pumps, changing the depth and penetration —the perfect combination of rough and tender.

"Yes," I cry out. Lost in sensations, I tremble and pant, barely able to hang on as I teeter on edge of ecstasy. I lift my hips, meeting and welcoming each thrust and as we come together, join as one, it occurs to me that what we're doing feels like a whole lot more than just two people fucking.

He buries his face in my neck. "You feel so good," he whispers, his tone low and husky. His voice vibrates through me, and my body lets go. I clench around his hard cock, my legs squeezing his punishing hips, as I tumble into a powerful orgasm. I claw at his back, each clench taking me higher and higher, until I'm soaring and Sean is soaring with me. He splashes high inside me, the long length of him throbbing and pulsing as he releases. I squeeze around him, lost in this moment, in Sean, and he moans. He presses kisses to my forehead, my nose, my chin and lips. His breath scorching my skin as we both fly high and free-fall back to earth. I hold him to me never wanting to let him go as our spasms stop. He eventually pulls out of me and rolls onto his back.

"Come here," he whispers, the soft warmth of his voice pulling me back. He breathes a sign of contentment, and with a great deal of tenderness, he pulls me to him, pressing his lips to my temple as he settles me against his chest. As he holds me, kisses me, possesses me, the things I feel for him rush over me like a windstorm. No matter how many times we make love, there is nothing he can do to douse the need, the flames inside me. When it comes to Sean, there is no way I can ever get enough.

"I'm in love with you, Summer," he says quietly, softly, and then drifts off to sleep.

My heart crashes as his words yank me back from fairy-tale land. The love I feel for him gathers like a knot in my gut, and worry eases itself into my bones.

I can no longer pretend this is just sex for me—or for him. It never was. Ever since I was a little girl, Sean represented safety, comfort, kindness, and compassion. All along he's known who I was, yet kept my secret. He's everything I want in a man and I'm in love with him and his family. But I'm in danger and that means I'm putting all of them in danger, too. Jack has many connections, a brotherhood of men on his side. The Owens boys might be tough and rough but they can't go up against a brotherhood—I would never ask them to—and what would I do if anything ever happened to one of them, to Gram, because of me.

I swallow. Hard. I made a mistake, a fatal flaw, by letting my guard down and letting Sean deep inside. The full impact of what I did, the danger I put this family in, hits like a blow. Jack could find me here, and hurt them. My last hope of finding the ledger died at the bus station. It's just not here— and neither should I be. As I mull that over, I draw a breath, knowing exactly what I need to do.

For the first time in a long time, I wake without a huge fucking knot in my stomach. These last two weeks have been a bitch, but last night with Summer, I can't even explain it. Making love to her helped chase my demons away. I still can't wrap my head around the fact that Dad had recorded all my races, and watched and rewatched them. If it wasn't for Summer I might never have learned that my dad was proud of me. My heart squeezes as I shift to my back and put my arm on my forehead. All this time, I had no idea he cared so much, was so proud of me. I might have fled Blue Bay with bad blood between us, but I think deep down he knew I loved him. Yeah, it sucks that I didn't make it back in time to tell him personally, but there is a part of me that believes he's looking down on us all, and maybe even smiling a bit—for once.

He would have liked Summer. Would have taken her in and treated her like the daughter he never had. A smile tugs at me. Gram sure loves her, and I'm not sure what they talked about when they went antiquing, but I'm guessing it has something to do with giving her grandkids.

I never thought I'd ever drive a minivan and have children. A sound catches in my throat. Jesus, I can't even believe that I'm caving and actually considering it now. What the fuck has Summer done to me? I'm not sure but I do know that if a minivan full of kids is what Summer wants, then that's what Summer gets.

I stretch and some part of me registers that the other side of the bed is dead quiet. I turn and when I find it empty, I sit up and wipe the sleep from my eyes. Where the fuck did Summer go? I check the clock, and while I'm surprised that it's nearing ten, I probably shouldn't be. The last few weeks have taken their toll on me and my weary body finally crashed hard.

I kick off the covers and stretch, expecting to find Summer in the shower, or kitchen, sucking back dishwasher coffee as she gets ready for work. Unless, of course, she'd already left. I pad through the quiet house, and Scout stirs in her bed and comes racing toward me. I pick her up and rub her behind the ears the way she likes.

"Hey, girl, where's your mom?" I go still, and play the word "mom" over and over in my head. *Summer a mom.* I kind of like the sound of it, actually. I laugh, a new lightness about me. How fucking crazy is it that I'm thinking about being a dad? I pull open the curtains, and don't really give a shit that I'm naked. I scan the beach, but Summer is nowhere to be found. She must have left for work already. I check the coffeepot and it's still hot.

"I guess I missed her, girl," I say to the squirming pup. "Okay, okay, let me just get my coffee and I'll take you out." I pour a big mug, tug on a pair of jeans, and open the front door. Scout darts for the grass, and as she sniffs around, I pull my cell from my back pocket and give Jared, one of the twins, a call. He's a master carver, a skill only he seemed to pick up from great-granddad when he was young, and I want him to make me something special for Summer, something that will help us move past the secrets and start fresh.

Scout finishes her business and darts inside. I follow her and check her bowls. There is still fresh water one of them, so I'm assuming Summer had fed her before going to work. I look around for a note, but don't find one. I'm a bit bummed by that. I sip my coffee and step into the living room. With Dad's funeral, I hadn't finished the floor yet. The new boards are still sitting in the box. I walk up to the damaged wall, and push the couch out of the way. My glance goes to the heater vent behind it, to the loose screws specifically.

I don't bother tightening them, the vent will have to be removed before I can plaster anyway. Scout scurries to the vent and sniffs like there's a fresh turkey cooking in there. Her tail wags double time.

"What's up, girl? Is there a mouse in there or something?" I set my coffee on the table, and work the loose screws with my fingers. They come out easily, which surprises me. The place has been locked up for years, and by rights these screws should have been seized in place. The knot in my stomach begins to tighten again, alarm bells jangling in the back of my brain as I remove the screws. I set them on the floor and ease the grate out. I lay it beside me, and Scout barks and sniffs the metal as I grab my phone from my back pocket and turn on my flashlight app. I peer inside the hole and what I see has my heart crashing and my buzzing brain coming to an abrupt halt. "No. Fucking. Way." I go back on my heels, and Scout darts for the hole. She puts two paws inside and starts barking.

I slide my hands around her chubby body, and pull her away. "It's okay, girl." I reach inside the hole, and pull out what looks like a small safe. I wince and press my nose to the crook of my arm to ward off a sneeze as I disturb the dust inside. "I think someone must have been here, not too long ago," I say to the dog, even though she has no idea what I'm talking about.

I bet Summer does.

Phone still in hand, I dial her cell, even though she told me not to. But I need to talk to her, now. My call goes to voicemail, instantly, and my gut clenches.

Jesus Christ, my mind starts working overtime, playing out every worst-case scenario that doesn't end well. I call Beck, a desperate sort of fear taking hold.

"Beck here," he says.

"Beck, it's Sean."

"Hey Sean, what's up?"

I try to keep my voice neutral. No sense in worrying everyone at this point. "I can't get hold of Summer. I tried her phone, but she must not have it with her. Can you grab her for me, ask her to call."

A moment of hesitation, then, "She didn't show up for work today, Sean."

Fuck. Fuck. Fuck.

"Is everything okay?" he asks.

I pinch the bridge of my nose and work to calm myself. "Yeah," I say, and end the call. My hands are shaking as I carry the safe to the kitchen counter. I check the lock, examine the keyhole. Goddammit, wouldn't you know it. Looks to me like that fucking key Summer carries fits in this lock. Fuck that. I walk to my toolbox. Grab a hammer and beat that fucking lock until it's broken.

Inside I find a manila envelope. I take it out and fold back the metal fastener. There appears to be a book of sorts inside. A noise sounds in the distance, and I go still, take in the quiet of the place. Every nerve I have is alive, my body tense, ready for a fight. I breathe deep, pull out the black book and flip through the pages. It's a ledger, with numbers—huge numbers—along with dates and names.

I have no idea what I'm holding, but my guess is Summer does.

I try her number again, panic exploding inside me. I need to find her and I need to do it now. I set Scout on her bed, shove the file into the back of my pants, jump into my truck and head through the city. When her big-ass truck is nowhere to be found I drive straight to Gram's. I hurry up the step and enter the house to find everyone sitting at the table. As soon as they see my face, every brother and cousin goes deadly still.

"What's wrong?" Jamie asks.

"Have you seen Summer?" I clench down hard enough to nearly break my back teeth, and drag my hand through my hair when all eyes stare at me, confused. "I mean Jenna."

Gram wipes her hands on her dishrag and steps up to me. "Is she in some kind of trouble?"

"Yes."

Chairs scrape and boots scuff as the guys climb to their feet and pile out of the house. "We'll help you find her," Ty says, and grabs his helmet. "Everyone spread out," he instructs.

I look at my own bike, and decide to take it instead of the truck. It will help me get around town easier. *Town?* Maybe she's already left town, is headed down Highway 2 on her way back to SoCal, and that's why I can't find her truck.

Shit. Shit. Shit.

Beads of sweat trickle down my back as I jump on my bike and tear through the streets. Fucking Walker will be all over me, but I don't give two shits right now. I need to find Summer. She's in trouble. Every instinct I have warns of it. As the guys search Blue Bay, I head toward the highway, leading to the next town. I wish I could convince myself that she went to Hope Falls for coffee, but that's bullshit and I know it. I hit the throttle, drive like the devil himself is chasing me and for all I know he is.

I round a sharp corner, and without warning I see Summer's truck, the front end steaming and crushed from a lethal, head-on collision with a guardrail. Momentarily paralyzed with terror, my heart punches into my throat. The soul-chilling sight sends a rush of adrenaline to my brain, and prompts me into action. Moving with breakneck speed, I jump from the bike, and bolt across the hot pavement at inhuman speed, terrified of what I might find inside. A pungent coppery scent clogs my nostrils when I reach the driver's side door, window crashed open. I look inside, and the sharp cry I hear is mine when I find her in the driver's seat—alive—rubbing her head, and fighting against the air bag. I touch her damp skin, needing the contact, to make sure I'm not imagining things.

It's been a long time since I've been afraid of anything. Heck, I'm all about taking risks, have a shit load of broken bones in my body, and skidded around hairpin turns that kill, but for the first time in my life, I know what real fear is.

"Summer," I say, and she shakes her head, then stills, and holds her hands to her ears like she's trying to get the world to stops spinning. Barely able to breathe, my chest begins to rise and fall in a panicky rhythm I can't seem to control. I open the door, and reach for her. "Summer, it's me, Sean," I say and she looks at me with confused eyes, blood dripping from her nose. "You were in an accident." I reach across her, grab a tissue from the box on the floor of the passenger side. "You hit the guardrail."

I hand her the tissue and she presses it to her nose. She blinks once, twice, then her eyes go wide as she looks behind us. Her breathing grows heavy, labored and her pulse jumps at the base of her throat. "You shouldn't . . . be here."

What the fuck?

She grips the steering wheel. "I need to go."

I crouch down to check on her, then hold my hand out. She eyes it tentatively. "You're not going anywhere. Your airbag has been deployed and you can't drive in the state you're in."

"You don't understand."

"What I don't understand is where you're going or what happened."

She looks down like she's trying to remember. "I was driving, then I tried to break for the corner, and I couldn't. Then I . . . I have to go, Sean." Full-blown panic edges her voice, bordering on hysteria.

I scan the ground, the trees hugging the highway. Anger, replaces worry. Why would she just take off? Yeah, I get she's in trouble, but she should have talked to me, asked me for her help. What, was I just a distraction, someone to occupy her time during her stay in Blue Bay? I thought we had more going on than that. Old fears rear their ugly head. Fuck, maybe she thought I wasn't good enough, that I'd only end up disappointing her.

"Sit here, don't move."

I walk to the front of the vehicle and drop down on to my back to look underneath. When I see the cut brake line, I jump to my feet. "We need to go. Now," I say and help her from the truck but when we turn, a car is slowing down behind us.

"Oh, God," Summer cries.

"What?"

"It's Jack."

"The ex?"

"Yes."

"What do I need to know, Summer?" I bite out, my voice harsh—dead fucking serious. The time for playing games is over. I need to know everything. "Tell me right now."

"Jack is a United States naval lieutenant. He worked under my dad for years and I think he might have been responsible for his death," she says quickly. "He's after something, Sean. A ledger. I think the key I found in the lockbox Dad gave me opens something, but I couldn't find it."

"I could," I say and push her behind me to shield her with my body.

"Well isn't that sweet," Jack say as he steps from the car and points a gun at us. "Looks like Summer went and found herself a bodyguard." He angles his head to take me in, his gaze traveling from my head to my boots, and I stand to my full height to square off against him. "Easy there, big guy. I'm not looking for trouble."

I breathe through the dread taking hold, needing to neutralize the situation before Summer gets hurt. "Then put the fucking gun down."

"I'll just be on my way, as soon as Summer gives me what I'm looking for."

"Jack, I have no idea where—"

"Then you're as stupid as your old man," he says, and I feel Summer go deadly still, her breath coming harder, pounding against my neck.

I widen my stance, a predatory move that has Jack angling his body, ready to go on the defense. Fuck, I should have pressed Summer, found out who this douchebag was earlier and hunted him down before it ever came to this. Why the fuck didn't she tell me how bad things were?

"I have what you're looking for," I say, wanting the attention on me, not Summer.

He smirks, his look dubious. "Is that right?"

"Yeah, that's fucking right."

He lifts the gun, points it between my eyes and Summer makes a yelping sound. "And what might I be looking for, asshole?"

"Black journal. Lots of names and numbers in it. If it ever ended up in the wrong hands . . ." I stop to give a slow whistle. "Looks like a lot of illegal activity going on. I think there would be all whole lot of shit coming your way."

His face hardens and he crooks his finger. "Hand it over. Or I'll kill you, like I killed her father."

Summer is shaking so hard behind me, it takes everything I have to concentrate on the gun and not turn around to console her. But I won't let anything happen to her. I'd fucking die first. "Oh, you think I'm stupid enough to have it with me?"

He shrugs. "Hey, I'm not judging your intelligence, despite the buttfuck hole of a town you live in. So just hand it fucking over, or I'll put one between your eyes."

"You do and you'll never find it."

"I'm getting tired of this game."

"I'll take you to it."

He smirks, slow and easy, and shakes his head, seemingly amused by me. Yeah, I might not be a naval lieutenant, but that doesn't mean I'm without my own resources.

"Sure, but Summer rides with me."

She tugs on my shirt. "No fucking way."

"Look, this doesn't involve you." He waves his gun. "Hand her over, and I'll make this real easy on you."

"I never was one for easy."

He stares at me, like he's trying to decide his next move. "Are you really willing to get yourself killed for her? You think because she spread her legs for you she wants you?" His laugh is cruel and harsh and Summer quivers, her fingers gripping my shirt so hard, I'm sure she's going to tear it. "You're a fucking redneck from Buttfuck, asshole. Apparently you are as fucking stupid as you look. It's called slumming, pal."

"That's not true," Summer whispers.

"You got something to say?" Jack asks.

"How did you find me?"

"You're not as smart as you think you are." He laughs. "A chip off the old block though. You never should have taken off, Summer. You just should have cooperated. Now your friend Susie has to get hurt."

Summer is crying behind me. "Jack, don't—"

"Too late for that."

"Why . . . how?" she asks, her voice boarding on hysteria.

"Little Susie called me last night. Reaching out to her was your first mistake. She made the second by calling me, worried about you. When I told her you broke your cell and I'd lost your number, she was happy to supply it. If you don't want anyone else hurt, you'd better give me what I want."

A burst of fury coils through me and my fingers curl into fists. If he's telling her about her friend, then he has no intention of letting us out of this alive. If I didn't think Summer would get hit in the crossfire I'd go straight for the guy's throat. As my mind races, catalogs my next move, a truck slows down behind Jack's car. I look past his shoulder, and feel a measure of relief when I see Jamie pulling to a stop behind the douchebag's car. Jamie jumps from his truck and gravel crunches beneath his boot. From his angle he can't see the gun. My brother has no fucking clue what kind of danger we're all in. This is bad. So fucking bad.

"What's going on?" he asks me.

Jack turns slightly at the sound, and acting purely on instinct, I rush him. No way is this douche going to hurt anyone I love. I kick the gun from his hand and land a hard one, right between his eyes. He goes down and I jump him, landing a few good right hooks to his face.

"Fucker," he says as he tries to kick me off. We fight, and he cracks my nose so hard, I'm sure it's broken. I shake my head as stars form, and he punches me in the gut, knocks the air out of me, and pulls a knife. He rolls me underneath him.

I grab his arm, hold the blade inches from my head, but the fucker is strong. Jamie runs, and kicks the knife from the guy's hand. Then the next kick is to the guy's head, and it knocks him out and off me.

"Keep him down," I say, and hold my gut, blood pouring from my nose as I climb to my feet. I turn to Summer, wipe my nose on my sleeve, and grab her hand, my main priority getting her to safety. "We need to go."

She nods, and I glance back to see Jamie on top of the guy, pinning him to the ground. Jack definitely messed with the wrong family, and I'm glad it was my fighter brother who came to our rescue. Jack might be a navy man, but Tyler is a tough cage fighter. No contest.

Summer hops on the back of the bike without question. I turn on the highway and go full throttle, my engine screaming as I race through town, every head turning my way. It's exactly what I want. Behind me Summer is holding on for dear life, but she doesn't have to worry. My bike is an extension of my body and I know exactly how to handle her. I fly down the streets, draw tons of attention as I cut through yards, my childhood days flashing before my eyes.

In no time at all I hear the cries of a siren. Summer squeezes my stomach. "Officer Walker," she warns.

If I wanted to I could have lost him, but him catching me is just what I had planned. I stop my bike and he climbs from his car, a look of victory on his face. He holds his hand over his gun.

"I knew it would only be a matter of time," he says, but his smile falters when he sees the blood.

I help Summer from the bike and hold my hands up. "I have something you're going to want to see. Something that's going to put your name on the map."

He eyes me, but he's not a stupid man. "What are you talking about?"

I slowly reach into the back of my pants and pull out the ledger. He takes it from me and opens it. "What the hell is this?"

"It's a ledger. Links to bank accounts and illegal activity, I believe." I look at Summer who is as equally surprised as Walker. "I found it at the Wheeler cottage. I think this is what got Colin Wheeler killed."

Walker's eyes go wide. "What are you talking about?"

"My real name is Summer Wheeler, and my dad's death wasn't an accident," Summer pipes up. "I've been on the run from my ex, Jack Kauffman." She points to the ledger. "He was after that. He found me because I made a call to a friend," she whispers, and looks at her feet. "She's in danger now, too."

"Who did you call?" Walker asks.

She gives her friend's name and number.

"I'll get an officer to her house," he says, and grabs his radio. He calls it in, then his cautious glance goes from me to Summer back to me again. "Where is this Jack?"

"You'll find him out on Highway 2. I believe Jamie has him detained."

Walker slaps the book against his hand. "I want to see both of you at the station. Don't think you're going anywhere anytime soon." I nod, and Walker jumps into his car.

I turn to Summer, my hands shaking so hard, my breath coming so fast, every emotion I've ever experienced hurling down on my like a big fucking eighteen wheeler.

I'm relieved, yet so fucking angry. How could she not have told me the danger she was in and why the fuck was she running away?

"Jesus, Summer." Her head jerks up at the gruffness in my voice. I'm so fucking mad, I'm practically spitting nails.

"Why did you make a fucking phone call?"

"I . . . I wanted to figure out how to help you get your

permits. I didn't think she'd call Jack. I'd been so careful, Sean."

I step away from her and suck in a sharp breath. Tearing fury rockets through me and I pace, running my hands through my hair, needing to punch something again. My gaze flies to her face, and anger takes hold. What if something had happened to her? My blood runs cold, penetrating my bones.

"Jesus fucking Christ, Summer. You put yourself in danger because of me. Don't ever fucking do that again." I pull my hair and kick at a rock. "Do you have any fucking idea how scared I was?"

"Sean . . ."

"You should have told me." I stop directly in front of her and her eye go wide. I take a moment to consider what she sees: a big fucking intimidating guy who is spitting mad at her. "Why didn't you tell me?"

"It was my problem not yours."

I shake my head, so fucking lost in her. An invisible band squeezes my heart. I love her. I fucking love her and I protect those I care about. I protect what's mine. If she doesn't know that by now—doesn't realize that I'll kill or be killed for her —it can only mean one thing.

She's not mine—and it's time we stop playing house.

SEAN

Three weeks has passed since I last saw Summer. After Walker took Jack into custody and questioned us, she disappeared, gone from Blue Bay in a flash. I only have myself to blame for that. Fucking asshole, I should have held my anger, shouldn't have lashed out at her the way I did. But I was so fucking angry that she didn't open up to me, trust me enough to tell me the kind of danger she was in. Now I'm angrier with myself.

I never pushed for answers and I played along with her fucking game, even calling her Jenna. I never should have done that. I should have gotten to the bottom of matters right from the start. Why didn't I? Oh, maybe because I'm an asshole and waited thirteen long fucking years for Summer to came back into my life and would have done anything she asked to keep her in it.

I stand inside her cottage and glance around at the finished floors and repaired wall. I run my hand over the new plaster. All that's needed is a fresh coat of paint. I step back, and Scout circles my feet. "I know, girl. I miss her, too." I look around, mourn Summer's absence, and work to ignore the hollow ache inside me. But the house feels fucking lonely without her.

I step into the kitchen and pour myself a cup of coffee. As I drink, my gaze goes to the sign I had Jared make when I thought Summer and I had a future together. It was my way of moving past the lies, but I never did give it to her.

A noise at the door heralds someone approach and I turn to see Gram. I love her, but I'm not really in the mood to talk to anyone. I've been pretty much holed up in the cottage since Summer left, finishing the work, despite the fact that she'd taken off for good.

"You did a great job," Gram says as she examines the floor and the walls.

"Thanks," I murmur feeling very little pride in the work.

She eyes me, and I brace myself. "Are you done sulking?"

"I'm not sulking."

She waves her hand at me. "I know sulking when I see it, Sean."

I push my hair off my face, every muscle in my body tense. "Gram . . ."

She holds her hand up to stop me and I go silent. "Haven't you had enough loss, Sean?"

I set my coffee cup on the counter and fold my arms. "She left, Gram. It was her decision. I had nothing to do with it."

"You don't think."

My mind takes that moment to race back to the cruel words I shot at her. I was so angry, so worried that Jack was going to hurt her and I wouldn't be able to stop him. I fist my hands and press them against my eyes.

"I was scared," I finally admit. "For the first time in my life I knew what real fear was."

"I know, Sean. But I also know she loves you." My hands fall, and Gram smiles.

"How do you know that?"

"She still looks at you today the same way she did all those years ago when you were racing through the streets and Officer Walker was chasing you." Gram gives a small laugh. "You really did give that man a run for his money."

True, I did. Walker locked Jack up, but he and his files were handed over to the NCIS, Naval Criminal Investigative Service, since it was a military case. The investigation is still ongoing, and after the news went national, and ran for days on CNN, Walker and I made an easy truce. News crews were here all week, but Walker ate that shit up. Me, well I just wanted to be left alone. Same as Summer. They camped out at her place, and she couldn't come or go without a camera in her face.

It's hard to believe Jack had been using Summer to find a ledger her father had hidden in the cottage. A ledger that identified all the men involved in using U.S. Navy ships to transport illegal cargo. Thank fuck the cops got to her friend Susie in time. Her house had been ransacked, Jack's men had been hunting for her, but she was working the night shift at the hospital and they hadn't gotten to her.

"Did you know right from the start Jenna was Summer?" I ask.

She nods. "Of course. But the big question is, why are you still here, Sean?"

I looked around the kitchen. "I started the job and I wanted to finish it," I say, my stomach sinking, sick to think the place will be abandoned for another thirteen long years.

"That's not what I mean and you know it." She picks up Scout, gives her a good rub behind the ears.

"Yeah, I know." What she's really asking is why I'm still here in Blue Bay and not in SoCal fighting for the girl I love.

"What if she doesn't—"

"Okay, come on, Sean. When have you ever given up without a fight?"

"Never," I say. So why the fuck am I doing it now? My blood rushes faster and I ball my fingers as I curse myself. She's the only girl I've ever loved, and I should have left a week ago. What if I'm too late? What if she's already moved on without me? Urgency moves through me, and my breath comes in a burst. "I need to go."

"I know."

I step up to Gram, give her a kiss on the cheek, but when I turn, ready to jump in my truck, and do whatever the fuck I need to prove to Summer that we belong together—even drive to her place in a damn minivan—my feet come to a resounding halt.

No. Fucking. Way.

I stand there for a moment, too astonished to breathe. "Summer," I finally say, my brain barely able to keep up as she brightens the doorway and lightens my dark mood.

"Sean," she says, and behind me, I hear the patio doors opening, and closing, Gram leaving with Scout to give us our privacy.

"I was . . . just . . . on my way . . ."

Her look is tormented as she tears her gaze from mine. "Can I come in?"

"It's your cottage," I say, and wave my hand for her to enter. She steps in, her eyes wide, appreciative as she takes in the finished floor and wall. "Everything looks beautiful." Her gaze goes to the sign Jared made. SUMMER WHEELER, CHIROPRACTOR.

"Can I get you a coffee?" I say for lack of anything else.

She gives me a small smile. "If that's what you insist on calling it." She follows me into the kitchen, and every nerve in my body is alive. I can't believe she's here. Did she come back because we had unfinished business? Or is she here to pack up her belongings and disappear for another thirteen long years?

I pour her a cup, put a splash of milk in it and hand it to her. She takes a sip and when she winces my heart soars with the love I feel for her.

"I . . ." we both begin at the same time.

"You go first," I say. She nods, pulls something from her purse, and hands it to me. "What's this?"

"The permit for the Cassidy house."

I try to swallow past the lump in my throat. "Is this why you came back? To give me this."

"Yes," she says and I turn from her. I look out the kitchen window, take a deep breath. "But it's not the only reason."

I spin back around. "No?"

She walks up to me, and holds her hand out. "I'm Summer Wheeler," she says. "I'm a chiropractor." He gaze goes to the sign. "But I guess you already know all that."

My hand swallows hers whole as I take it into mine. "Sean Owens," I say. "Motocross racer turned handyman."

"Handyman, huh?"

"Yeah."

She takes my hands and the clean scent of her soap washes over me. "So you're good with your hands."

Need gathers in the pit of my stomach as she touches me. "I am."

"Confident, I like that."

I stare at her, take in the vulnerability in her eye and my heart squeezes so tight in my chest, my throat closes over. "Summer, what are we doing?"

"We're starting again, Sean. The way we should have started a month ago."

I brush my thumb over her cheek. My heart crashing so hard in my chest, it rings in my ears. "Why didn't you tell me how much trouble you were in? You know I protect what's mine."

"I didn't know I was yours," she says quietly.

I shake my head, and briefly pinch my eyes shut. "How could you not know that?"

"I wanted it so much, Sean. I wanted you. Your family. I wanted it all. But I was scared. I was too scared to tell you anything because Jack's contacts ran deep. He and his army friends are a brotherhood, and I didn't want anything to happen to you or your family. I could never live with myself if anyone of you got hurt because of me."

I take in the shadows under her eyes. She doesn't look to be sleeping any better than me. "You were protecting . . . me?"

"Yes."

As all the pieces come together, I nod. "Okay," I say. "I get it, but you do realize I can protect myself right, and I come with my own army."

She gives me a wobbly smile. "Yes. I realize that now."

"Why did you leave?"

"You were so angry, Sean. I wasn't sure you wanted me to stay."

I grip my hair and pull it. Fuck. "I'm sorry. I didn't mean to get so angry, but I was scared, Summer. I'd never been that scared in my fucking life."

"I was scared, too. Still am."

I pull her to me, and glance over her shoulder expecting to see someone holding a gun over us. "Why?"

"I'm scared I ruined things between us. You see, Sean. I've loved you since I was twelve years old."

I nearly sob from happiness. "I've loved you just as long, Summer."

"I never should have thought I could trick you into believing I was someone else."

"It might have been thirteen years, but the second I set eyes on you I knew who you were."

"Same, but it hasn't been thirteen years for me."

"No?"

"Dad and I watched all your races. We were so proud of our Blue Bay boy."

My head rears back. "Your dad . . . proud of me?" I scoff and wave my finger between us. "I'm not sure he'd be so happy about this."

"I thing you might be wrong about that. I think he knew how protective you were of me and might have sent me here on purpose."

While I'm not too sure about that, there's a question I need to ask, even though I'm not sure I want to hear the answer. "How long are you here?"

"Seeing as you went through all the trouble to make a sign for me. The least I could do is stay and open my practice. Besides you won't go to a doctor and you need someone to help you work all the kinks out," she says, her voice playful, so mischievous my insides warms, aching to take her to the bedroom and show her just how much I like that idea.

"There you go using that word 'kink' again. Don't toy with me, Summer. There will be consequences." She grins like she likes that idea and my heart soars with the love I have for her. But I wipe all playfulness away and sober. "Only one problem, though."

She angels her head, take in the seriousness on my face. "A problem?" she asks, and takes a tentative step back, like she's worried she really did make a mess of things. "What kind of problem?"

"As far as I'm concerned, we need to toss that sign in the garbage."

She gulps and I hear her throat. "Sean, I thought—"

"It has your name wrong."

"I know I never should have said I was Jenna—"

"Summer," I say, stopping her. "It has your last name wrong."

She still looks confused, until I drop down onto one knee. Her eyes go wide and her mouth drops open forming that perfect "O" that I love so much.

"It should say Summer Owens."

"Sean—"

"Marry me, Summer. Make me the happiest man in the world."

She takes deep gulping breaths, tears pooling in her eyes. "Say yes."

"Yes," she cries out, and I climb to my feet, gather her into my arms and carry her down the hall.

"Now there are only two things left."

"What?" she asks as she wraps her arms around me to hang on. And she'd better fucking hang on because we only get one shot at this life, and ours is going to be a ride to remember. "The cottage is finished, and it's time to for us to christen it."

She giggles, and presses her mouth to mine. I kiss her with all the love inside me. I set her on the bed and tug off my T-shirt. Her eyes roam over my scars, ones that have healed from her love and her touch, then her eyes go wide. "Wait, you said two things."

"That's right. We need to work on giving Gram that little great-granddaughter she wants."

Summer's smile nearly brings tears to my fucking eyes. She reaches out to me, pulls me to her warm body. "I love you Sean."

"I love you, too, Summer," I say as I close my lips over hers. "I always have."

AFTERWORD

Thank You!

Thank you so much for reading, **Demolished**, book 1 in my Blue Bay Crew Series. I hope you loved this story as much as I loved writing it. Be sure to check out the second Book **Leveled**. Keep reading for an excerpt of **Leveled.**

Interested in leaving a review? Please do! Reviews help readers connect with books that work for them. I appreciate all reviews, whether positive or negative.

Happy Reading,

Cathryn

Jamie

Trouble in a bikini.

Yeah, that's what I see from my rooftop vantage point. Trouble in a goddamn bikini, and I don't plan to get within fifty feet of a pretty little rich girl like her. Been there, done that, and have the scars to prove it.

Literally.

I squeeze my fingers around the hammer in my fist, my thoughts racing back to when I was eighteen, specifically to the day I received the shit-kicking of a lifetime. All thanks to a girl no different than the one below me, spread out on her chair without a care in the world as she tans her hot body under the scorching noonday sun.

What I'd do to come face-to-face with my ex's asshole brothers today. Four against one. Yeah, they waited until I was alone and jumped me. Fucking cowards, really. Too afraid of a fair fight, or of facing off against me and my army of brothers. At least I have the satisfaction of knowing I'd broken a few of their noses and cracked a few of their ribs. I can almost hear the bones crunching now.

"Come on, Jamie, you can't tell me you don't want to tap

that," my cousin Ryan says as the blonde shades the sun from her eyes and glances at us before climbing from her lounge chair. I'm pretty sure she just gave an extra shake to her sweet ass as she made her way inside her beachside cottage. Cottage? Okay, more like mansion. Whatever. Doesn't make a difference to me, and she can shake her ass all she wants. That's wasted on me too.

Mostly.

I ignore my twitching cock and with the back of my hand I wipe the perspiration from my forehead and turn to glare at Ryan. "Tap that? No fucking way." I shake my head. Christ, of all the guys—my four brothers and three cousins included—Ryan knows my motto better than any of them: Avoid rich pampered women at all costs. Fuck, man, he was the one who found me in the alleyway and picked my broken and bloodied body up off the ground, all because I messed around with the wrong girl.

A sound catches in my throat. Wrong girl? More like a bored little rich girl who spent the summer slumming with a boy from the wrong side of the tracks, only to end up accusing me of rape when her father walked in on us. Talk about a shit storm of courts and chaos that followed me around after that.

To think I was so young and naïve—stupid really—the two of us talking about a future together. Christ, I was such a fucking dreamer back then. Even my father would get on my case about it. How many times did I drift off in thought when Dad was teaching me construction techniques? Too many to count, that's for sure. But none of that mattered in the end. After the charges were dropped, I left Blue Bay, my days of dreaming and trusting over, but a dark cloud still hangs over my head here in the town where I grew up.

The long-term summer vacationers, who continue to come back year after year from all over the states, will always treat me like I'm a fucking criminal, and I would have stayed in New Orleans for good if my brother Sean hadn't insisted I return home to help with the business after our dad died. I'm doing my part, but that doesn't mean I have to like it. Truthfully, I don't hate it. I had a hammer in my hand before I could fucking talk. We all did. It's just that I prefer the art of tattooing to construction. At least I have my nights and weekends off, and I was able to buy a small space on the other side of town—where the privileged, self-righteous vacationers never venture. Good. I don't need their business, or their support, when I finally get it up and running.

"She's all yours, bro," I say to my cousin Ryan, who'd also returned home at my big brother Sean's insistence. He was a mechanic down in Georgia, but gave it all up in the name of family. "But take my advice, she's got trouble written all over her, and if I were you, I'd stay as far away from her as possible."

He clucks his tongue and grabs another stack of roofing shingles. He sinks to his knees and pulls a few nails from his tool belt. "Yeah, you're probably right. Who needs that kind of shit in their life, anyway?"

"I sure as hell don't," I say. "Not again." But when I hear a loud shriek coming from the neighboring house—the hot blonde's cottage—every muscle in my body tightens.

"What the fuck?" Ryan asks. He stands and walks over to the edge of the roof with me. Shoulder to shoulder, we go still and listen, but when another loud cry sounds, it prompts me in to action.

"Son of a bitch." I kick my leg out and hurry down the ladder. Ryan's boots echo on the metal rungs as he follows, and he stays tight on my heels as we race to the cottage next door. I peer through her screen door, and even though every instinct I have warns me to run the other way, I was raised better than that, and when push comes to shove, it's not in my nature to turn my back on someone who might need my help. Pampered rich girl or not.

"You okay?" I ask from the other side of the door, and count to three as I wait for an answer. When none comes, I exchange a quick look with Ryan and pull on the handle. With my luck I'll probably get accused of breaking and entering, but I yank it open anyway, worry for the girl's well-being gnawing at my gut. The hinges, rusty from the saltwater spray, groan as I stretch them. "Hello," I call out, and step into the house, which smells like coconut suntan lotion—a scent that takes me back to my days in bed with the girl who fabricated a lie that will forever haunt me.

A loud bang, like something—or someone—is being smashed against the wall, reverberates through me, and without thinking I hurry toward the sound, my work boots scuffing on the polished wood floor. But I'm seriously fucking worried she's being attacked, and I'm not about to stop to take my boots off to save her precious oak from getting damaged. I turn the corner, stop at a bedroom to do a quick scan, but all I see is a sewing machine, a dummy with a dress draping off it, and spools of threads and material everywhere. I continue down the hall and stop at the second bedroom. I grip the doorframe and air leaves my lungs in a whoosh when I see what all the commotion is about.

Fuck. Me. Hard.

I want to turn. I should turn. Actually, I should bolt, leave Blue Bay, Connecticut, for good this time, and never look back. But I don't do any of those things. How the fuck could I possibly think of running when I'm staring at the hottest, most gorgeous naked body I've ever set eyes on? Unable to help myself, I give a fast sweep over her nakedness, taking in her long legs, curvy hips, and small breasts that would fit so nicely in my big hands, or better yet, my mouth.

"Jamie," Ryan says, crashing into me, pushing me a little

farther into the bedroom. I stumble and quickly right myself, but not before I get a whiff of the girl's scent. I breathe in her sweet floral aroma, and it strokes my thickening dick, teases and tortures my last working brain cell. Why again is it I don't do pampered rich girls?

"Oh, shit, sorry," Ryan says, when he glimpses the girl scrambling for her robe, and my thoughts come crashing back to the present.

This time I do look away, and grab Ryan's shoulders to turn him too. "Sorry," I say quickly. "We heard a scream. I thought you were in trouble. Didn't mean to walk in on you like this."

"I . . . it was a spider," she says, her voice as sweet and seductive as the woman herself.

Get your shit together, dude. She's everything you vowed to stay away from.

The whoosh of silk fills the silence as she dresses, and I can't help but envy that robe as it gets to touch her body, shape her curves, slide between her legs.

I'm envying a fucking robe?

"You can turn now," she says quietly.

I slowly inch around, and her blue eyes are wide, alarmed, as her gaze goes from me to Ryan, back to me again. I take a minute to see the situation through her eyes and can understand why she looks so frightened. She's just a tiny thing and both Ryan and I are big men, over six feet and covered in tattoos. We're dressed only in jeans, boots and tool belts, and we're blocking her bedroom doorway. Fuck, if I were her, I'd be scared shitless too. But she has nothing to worry from us. Despite our reputation—poster boys for authority issues—we know right from wrong.

Mostly.

Her gaze leaves mine and travels downward, raking over my bare chest like a hot caress. The fear in her eyes changes to appreciation, and my dick twitches again. Fuck, man, I wish she wasn't looking at me like that. It's making it harder and harder for me, and yeah, when I say harder, I'm talking about my dick. Needing a distraction, I glance away and see shattered glass on her floor.

I clear my throat and hope her gaze stops at my tool belt. No need for her to see my hard-on and get the wrong idea that I might want her. I don't.

"Did you get it?"

"Get what?" she asks, her voice sounding more breathless.

My gaze meets hers again. "The spider."

"Oh." She turns toward the glass. "I hit it with my figurine."

A figurine that probably costs more than I make in a week.

"All right. Everything seems good. Glad you're okay. We'll get out of your way."

I turn, and Ryan is grinning at me. Little fucker knows the girl is getting to me. I give him a shove to set him in to motion, and he walks back into the other room. I'm about to follow when she says, "Can I get you a drink? You look hot . . . I mean, it's hot out and you've been on that roof all morning."

I swallow against a dry throat. "No, I'm good."

"I'm Kylee."

I nod and walk out to the main room, but Ryan is long gone, leaving the two of us alone. Motherfucker. I'm going to kill him.

"And you are . . . ?" she probes.

Leaving.

I scrub my chin again, and as much as I just want to get the hell out of there, I was raised with manners. I know one wouldn't think it to look at me. Christ, I hung out with the toughest bastards in New Orleans, fought alongside the meanest gangs, yet I still don't want to be rude to this girl.

"Jamie."

"Nice to meet you, Jamie. Thanks for coming to my rescue."

"Jamie Owens," I say and wait for a reaction, for it to ring a bell. In two seconds I expect a light bulb to go off and her to shove me out the door.

"Kylee Jensen," she says instead.

Guess she doesn't know the Owens boys' reputation. I suppose that shouldn't surprise me. This cottage just sold, and she's new to the area. She's awfully young to own such a big, expensive place on the ocean, though. Either she has a high-paying job, or Daddy bought it for her. I'm going with the latter. And soon enough she'll learn who I am. When all the regular vacationers return next month or so, she'll be warned away from me and won't dare shake her ass at me or invite me into her house again.

Until then, however . . .

What the fuck?

Until then, I still plan to avoid her.

I just hope Grandma Nellie doesn't take it upon herself to invite the newcomer to any Sunday dinners. She's been known to do that. If she does, I plan to make myself scarce.

Kylee steps up to me and zeroes in on my sugar skull tattoo. She puts her finger on my body and I flinch. Her eyes go wide again and she pulls her hand back fast.

"Sorry." She shakes her head. "I shouldn't have touched you."

"It's fine."

She eyes me for a second, then puts her fingers back on me. Sweet fuck, her fingers are so goddamn warm and soft as she traces the skull tattoo, I can't help but want them on my dick.

"This one is really nice," she says.

"Thanks. I designed it for a client when I owned my shop in New Orleans. Liked it so much, I gave myself one."

Why the fuck am I telling her that?

Her hand drops to her side, and she puts it on her hip. "Wow, a real artist. I'm impressed."

"You should be."

She grins, and despite myself, I grin too. "Modest, I like that," she teases and tightens her robe around her sweet curves. "I almost got a tattoo when I turned eighteen, but my father, the all-powerful Jack Jensen, threatened to disown me."

I nod. "Fathers are protective like that."

She angles her head and her soft curls fall down her slender shoulder. Jesus fuck, what I'd do to twist those long strands around my palm as I fuck her bent over her sofa.

"You sound like you know firsthand."

"I've had a few come into my shop, ready to kill me after inking their daughters. But I don't ink underage girls, and they have to be sober. Still, some fathers want to challenge me."

She frowns, and the deep sadness on her face is like a punch to the gut. What did I say to upset her? And why the fuck does seeing her upset bother me so much?

"That's what my father would have done." She wipes away the sorrow and smiles, but it's forced. Ah, I get it. Daddy issues. All the more reason for me to keep my distance. "He's a bit overprotective." Her big eyes race over my naked chest again.

"There are ways to get around that, you know," I say.

"Yeah?"

My gaze drops, lingers at the juncture between her thighs. "Places to ink where he'll never see."

What the fuck am I doing?

When my gaze returns to hers, there is a pink flush on her

cheeks. It's been a long time since I've seen a girl blush. Damned if it isn't sexy as fuck. She looks over my body again, her eyes questioning.

"What?" I ask.

"I . . . uh . . . was just wondering . . ." She shakes her head. "Nothing. Never mind."

Don't ask, dude. Don't ask. Just leave.

"Wondering what?"

Dammit

"Just . . . where did you put your girl's name?"

I hook my thumbs into my tool belt, needing to restrain my hands before I do something I could only regret later. You know, like pull her to me and see if those lips taste as sweet as they look.

"Nowhere." I don't elaborate, don't tell her ink is permanent and relationships aren't—at least for me they aren't. I'm an Owens. The kind of guy a girl fucks, not one she brings home to Daddy. Especially a protective one like hers.

She toys with the silk belt on her robe. Jesus, one tug and she'd be naked again. "You sure you don't want a drink? It's the least I could do after you ran to my rescue."

The least.

"I'm good." Good? No, not really. I got a fucking monster boner, and that's not good at all. I'm all about fucking, just not girls like her. Jesus, man, I need to get back to work and get back to minding my own business before things take a turn for the worse and I act on my fucking urges. Seems to me like she wants me to, though, from the way she's eye fucking me and all and asking if I have a girl. But I'm done with bored women looking to spice up their dull lives with a little danger. I don't trust her, but more importantly, I don't trust myself around her.

"I better get back to work," I say.

"Before you go, can I . . . ah . . . show you something?"

Yes, please...

I open my mouth, afraid of what's going to come out—yeah, all the blood is in my dick—but I pinch my lips shut when she points toward the ocean. "I was thinking my back deck needs to be replaced. It's pretty weathered. Hang on." She darts to her kitchen, her sweet ass dragging my focus, and comes back with a piece of paper. "I was thinking something like this."

I take the paper from her and look at the drawing. "You sketched this?"

She nods. "Impressed?"

"Very."

"You should be."

I can't help but smile. Beautiful and witty. A dangerous combination.

Like I said, trouble in a bikini, and I'd be wise to remember that.

I tug a business card from my back pocket and hand it to her. "My brother Sean will check it out and give you a quote."

She reads the print, then flicks the card against her hand. "Blue Bay Construction. Concise. To the point. I like that."

Yeah, and I like her.

Fuck me twice.

"Sean will find the right man for the job."

"Oh, I thought you—"

"Busy next door," I say, even though the job is almost done. "But if you want my opinion, I'd go with composite next time. The salt water is a bitch, and you'll end up replacing the wood in another ten years."

"Good plan. Thanks. I'll give your brother Sean a call, or maybe I'll stop in to see him. I have to run to town anyway." I turn to leave, and she says, "See you soon, Jamie."

Not if I fucking see her first.

ALSO BY CATHRYN FOX

Blue Bay Crew
Demolished
Leveled
Hammered

Single Dad
Single Dad Next Door
Single Dad on Tap
Single Dad Burning Up

Players on Ice
The Playmaker
The Stick Handler
The Body Checker
The Hard Hitter
The Risk Taker
The Wing Man
The Puck Charmer
The Troublemaker
The Rule Breaker

In the Line of Duty
His Obsession Next Door
His Strings to Pull
His Trouble in Talulah
His Taste of Temptation

His Moment to Steal

His Best Friend's Girl

His Reason to Stay

Confessions

Confessions of a Bad Boy Professor

Confessions of a Bad Boy Officer

Confessions of a Bad Boy Fighter

Confessions of a Bad Boy Gamer

Confessions of a Bad Boy Millionaire

Confessions of a Bad Boy Santa

Confessions of a Bad Boy CEO

Hands On

Hands On

Body Contact

Full Exposure

Dossier

Private Reserve

House Rules

Under Pressure

Big Catch

Brazilian Fantasy

Improper Proposal

Boys of Beachville

Good at Being Bad

Igniting the Bad Boy

Bad Girl Therapy

Stone Cliff Series:

Crashing Down

Wasted Summer

Love Lessons

Wrapped Up

Eternal Pleasure Series

Instinctive

Impulsive

Indulgent

Sun Stroked Series

Seaside Seduction

Deep Desire

Private Pleasure

Captured and Claimed Series:

Yours to Take

Yours to Teach

Yours to Keep

Firefighter Heat Series

Fever

Siren

Flash Fire

Playing For Keeps Series

Slow Ride

Wild Ride

Sweet Ride

Breaking the Rules:

Hold Me Down Hard

Pin Me Up Proper

Tie Me Down Tight

Stand Alone Title:

Hands on with the CEO

Torn Between Two Brothers

Holiday Spirit

Unleashed

Knocking on Demon's Door

Web of Desire

ABOUT CATHRYN

New York Times and *USA today* Bestselling author, Cathryn is a wife, mom, sister, daughter, and friend. She loves dogs, sunny weather, anything chocolate (she never says no to a brownie) pizza and red wine. She has two teenagers who keep her busy with their never ending activities, and a husband who is convinced he can turn her into a mixed martial arts fan. Cathryn can never find balance in her life, is always trying to find time to go to the gym, can never keep up with emails, Facebook or Twitter and tries to write page-turning books that her readers will love.

Connect with Cathryn:
Newsletter https://app.mailerlite.com/webforms/
landing/c1f8n1
Twitter: https://twitter.com/writercatfox
Facebook: https://www.facebook.com/
AuthorCathrynFox?ref=hl
Blog: http://cathrynfox.com/blog/
Goodreads: https://www.goodreads.com/author/show/
91799.Cathryn_Fox

Pinterest http://www.pinterest.com/catkalen/